Seven Eleven Forgotten and Other Stories

by Barnaby Hazen

The Stories

You know who you are, and thanks.

Seven Eleven Ceremony

I was lost in Los Angeles wondering where I might buy an L.A. map. Maps seem to be passé, and often it's just as things are phasing out I decide to become an expert on them.

Out of the bushes, I heard a rugged voice. He was sitting on a curb hidden by the foliage when he said, "It wouldn't hurt my feelings if you gave me some change on the way out." That was Aaron from the Wrecking Crew; a borderline gang of white middle aged ex-cons, more on them later. I introduced myself by first and middle name, Alex Aronovich, to Aaron, something completely unnecessary and probably unwise, but like I say, more on that later.

The money in Aaron's pitch was that it wouldn't "hurt his feelings" to get some help. So many of us find it insulting when people offer us help. He was opening up to the passerby, in a way. Among friends I have been drinking with, breaking off to hang with homeless people is also just starting to fall out of vogue.

But with maps—years ago, when I briefly aimed to become a cab driver here in Los Angeles, I failed based on my inability to read a map under pressure. Pressure was my downfall, looking up directions was easy. During the in-class test, I beat the entire class and even thought a few of those students were envious of me. We were using the bible of cabbies, a Houghton Mifflin publication, to look up ten destinations. Cabbies are very competitive, knowing the range of pay is broad, and the difference between the highest and lowest paid is savvy and speed. I liked our trainer, but when it was time for a road test, we got a new trainer. He was a weird guy with a bad redhead hairpiece and he played a recording of, "Tie a Yellow Ribbon 'Round the Old Oak Tree" as a selling pitch that we had "found a home" in these yellow cabs.

When the new trainer with the piece tested me on the road, I lost all of my savvy—I froze completely. He talked me through the same steps for finding a location with the map the previous trainer had, but I still took three times as long, and at one point I even had the Yellow Ribbon trainer shaking his head when I was about to make a turn, pointing the opposite way in quiet exasperation. "Alex, it's that way. No—no turn around up there."

I remember afterward feeling just like I had after the swim test I took when I was at the YMCA as a kid. I had been swimming for three years, but started weeping mid-pool for my test, either because the water was colder than I was used to, I was being tested by strangers, or what have you. Just bobbing around, pissing and farting in the water and feeling like a complete ass in the shallow end for an entire hour of swimming pool time gave me plenty of opportunity to think about why I hadn't been able to swim that very easy distance, when weeks before I had taken long swims from one beach to another in the ocean—a swimming feat my parents were both vocally uncomfortable with. I also considered trying to retake the test, all the while feeling like a lower class citizen stuck with the kids who either said they couldn't swim, or like me, had made the staff believe they couldn't swim by failing that test. "Marco..."

In any case, I have been studying the L.A. map book ever since. I have practiced it theoretically, using it on random "to and from" cross-streets maybe once every couple of weeks, and brought it with me each of the many times I've driven down from Portland, Oregon where I now reside with Jake (an expert on Los Angeles 7-Elevens, more on him later) and his wife Tatiana. I have even given myself new destinations and deadlines aiming to simulate the kind of pressure that threw me off that miserable day I failed my cabbie road test. Back then I could smell Yellow Ribbon's underarm deodorant and recognize it as my roommate's same exact brand, an impressive distinction under pressure; but to my most pressing duty of finding my way to somewhere near the taxi station, I was useless.

When the real call comes, that all family members need to come to see someone before his time is up, you forget things. You are baffled by the conversations, and how everyone gets at each other and quibbles as if it's just normal life until someone breaks into tears, and then magically gains the sympathy of everyone near. So my map-book is probably right next to my computer.

In any case, I left 7-Eleven empty handed. They don't even have a foldout map of Los Angeles. My rental has a GPS I have given up on. I could shoot for verbal directions combined with blind luck and probably still miss my father's funeral with his abrasive voice running through my head while looking for it: "This GPS is shit! Pull over, I don't like the way this is going!"

And now I am learning that the little clique Aaron calls the Wrecking Crew is in need of someone to buy liquor for them at this store. Aaron and associates were refused just yesterday, you see.

And Aaron already knows my first and middle name, and that my father gave me my middle name based on his first, Aron, in the Russian tradition of taking one's father's first as a patronymic. And these guys looked at me funny for using the word "patronymic," but they did not seem to object to my level of education much once the beer was purchased and circulating. And Aaron has some words of wisdom, like when it's time to head to the campground, even though his Native American friend wants to go pan-handle and get some more beer, and the elephant on the corner so to speak is that I am obviously a little better off than the rest of us here so I offer to buy more while they stay back; but the other Anglo beefy looking serious ex-con with serious ex-con type tats comes with to make sure no one bothers me (or to make sure I come back at all). I ask him what's with all the jokes about anal rape, and he says it's just them having a good time, just prison humor, and this gets more attention than I would have liked as we get back and he's telling everyone, "Hey homeboy here was worried we was gonna *rape* him!" and everyone laughs and reintroduces themselves saying, "Hi I'm so-and-so and I ain't no fag," and I don't really believe a confrontation is out of the scope of possible endings here, but figure I know how to box my way out and run when it's time. Eventually I say I've missed my dad's funeral, and that I'm taking one of the forties with me now since I'm leaving and at first Aaron doesn't acknowledge me, then he sounds impatient, impatient in a manner strangely similar to my late dad as he says, "I said it's okay!" And everybody has a round of jokes about what useless pieces of shit their dads were, and I don't join in much because I got past that and got to see him as he was, once he kicked drinking, and I have to admit that drinking does seem to be where a lot of people's problems end up. They may not start there, but they do end up there.

I think these guys didn't have dads who cried as much as mine did. I mean not like everyday but at least three times when I was less than ten years old I felt like trying to help my dad because he was weeping over our cats that got run over, or he was making some remarkably irresponsible statement like, "What the fuck do you need me for?" while crying and it occurs to me that probably all of us drink when we don't want to ask for help, then we're up to our ears in more than we can handle and drinking until we don't have any choice we figure but to break down in front of someone who definitely shouldn't be the one you're finally asking for help.

And the GPS gets me to my room, the forty gets me to sleep, and I'm an expert on old drunks like my dad, now that another one has fallen out of vogue forever.

The Sweet Tooth and the Coin Collection

Whether Lisa was at home or at Grandad's, Mom gave her the same deal on Saturday: she could have more than one sweet in a day. Her favorite way of taking advantage of this was to get a handful of Red Vines and a Big Gulp. She would then bite the ends off of the licorice sticks and use them as straws to drink her soda, occasionally wolfing down the rest of her "straw" to move on to the next Red Vine and make another. The problem was that her little cousin Ben was at Grandpa's too. Ben would always take these plans too far and risk getting everything taken away by Grandpa, to be dealt with as per Mom's discretion after dinner. The sodas wouldn't be any good by then, and without those she would be drinking water or orange juice or something else in the 'fridge with her Red Vines, an experience not nearly as wickedly enjoyable as the one she had in mind.

If she sold Ben on the packaged Red Vines instead of the ones they had in those big plastic containers up front somehow, she might be able to keep the number of candy sticks at least looking fairly sensible to Grandpa or other adults. Those were only 10 cents each, while those in packages she remembered as being closer to three dollars a pack. If each of them had a pack, they wouldn't necessarily get all over the place attracting attention.

With this strategy in mind, she addressed her cousin: "You know what I'm gonna get? I'm gonna get Red Vines."

"Cool!"

"But not those ones up front."

"Mm mm!" Ben shook his head seriously, already going along with Lisa's plan, though he didn't know what Lisa was going to say.

"The ones in the packages taste way better."

"Way better. I'm gonna get those too!"

Meanwhile Grandpa Nate was preoccupied with the new album he'd gotten to hold the coins from his centennial quarter collection, among others. The buffalo pennies and nickels, and the gold coins that had always been pushing the perimeters out, and breaking the plastic envelopes in his old albums were finally going to a new home, and this was the day he would at least have a chance to move them into new spots, perhaps only temporarily.

"Grandad, we're going to the store!"

"Okay, take your cell phone!"

"I will—bye!"

"See you soon."

The pennies were well placed to the back of the album. There were larger slots in the middle for the eagle and half eagle gold coins, though he had to split them up in a few awkward groupings. The front of the album was where he intended to put the error coins, quarters mostly, all of which were in quarter rolls from the bank, temporarily while he waited for this very opportunity to find them homes among the rest of this collection. He went back into his den, saw the desk open and at first only mused with himself at the very idea, but soon found one of those very quarter rolls broken into for candy, presumably, by Lisa and Ben, who had left merely four of those unique quarters behind along with the roughly torn paper that had been the quarter roll. Altogether the roll was worth, as he counted it, roughly five thousand dollars if he put some time into selling them, which was never his intention.

Furious, he remained in his den and seated for several minutes sorting out a plan. He would let the kids know they needed to respect his den and anything in it, but they had taken money from there with his blessing before, so how would he differentiate, between those days and this remarkable loss? He could take them both to see the clerk asking to sort through those quarters in spite of the fact that he had relinquished possession of them unintentionally with the help of his adorable grandchildren; but they would know they had done something wrong. From that moment, Ben would be sure to let Mom in on it, who would call Grandpa Nate wound up as could be, and no matter how Nate might try to downplay the loss, there would probably be spankings involved, maybe even grounding, so no visits for a while.

Numb, he walked out to where the kids were watching TV: "What are you watching?" he asked with no interest.

"Sponge Bob, the movie!" they said, a little irritated that he would interrupt with such a question.

He had a harder time getting his next two questions out, "Do you have any change?"

"Yeah," Lisa said, as she chomped on a Red Vine she had just pulled out of her soda. "Over there," and she pointed with the same Red Vine at two of those quarters and some utterly worthless change from the store on top of a low shelf on the entertainment center.

"How is the candy?"

"Good," said Lisa, looking briefly at him and smacking with so much vigor that it seemed to Nate he could probably hear her smacking from absolutely anywhere else in the house.

"Well," said Nate, "that's good to hear. Can I have one?"

Both kids laughed at that, "Of course not, Granddad! You don't eat Red Vines."

"Yeah," he sighed, "I think it's time I finally tried one."

Crash, Seven Eleven!

Alex was sleeping in the upstairs room because he had been on the computer watching movies until about 3 a.m. At around 4:40, he heard a sound he at first thought was a gun, then felt the house move and thought he was in an earthquake. It shook, he got up and looked out the window and assumed the house would be toppling over until his eyes finally made sense of the police lights outside, and he squinted to put together more details:

Half of a car was in the living room below him, while the other half was being yelled at by two Marina del Rey police officers with their guns drawn. Alex couldn't figure out how to proceed. He thought that an intruder was now below him, might be armed, and he considered Jake's guns, then realized that the police were ready to shoot and didn't really know who he was or that he was staying there, house-sitting. He could run downstairs to see the car, but he'd have to be careful about how he introduced himself to the scene. Where was the driver? Was he still in the car, armed, fixing to move to the staircase and start his last stand gunfight upstairs? Alex was thinking he could stick his head out the window, but then where was Jake's old dog, Betsy? He thought he remembered hearing barking at first, but was suddenly very nervous for Betsy's well-being.

For the first time in his life, Alex found he was relieved to hear commands from police officers, such as "Get down on the floor, hands above your head!" because this implied the culprit was not headed for him. He waited until everything sounded well under control before he called down, "Hello? Don't shoot, I'm a resident."

Once the police had seen Alex's driver's license and ran his plates they showed such marginal interest in him or the house that Alex was shocked into wondering if Jake might have a lawsuit of his own against the police. They shouldn't have been involved in a high-speed chase in a residential area in the first place, and as Alex was piecing it back together for himself, the crash and the police lights seemed practically one right after another—meaning the police had to be involved in a high speed chase despite what they told him, that they were following the young driver at a considerable distance. The incarceration of the 19 year-old kid (also called Alex, Alex noticed) seemed their sole concern and they left quickly with their prisoner satisfied that Alex (not their prisoner) would call the true owner of the house, Jake, who might then call his insurance company.

The phone wasn't working, maybe circuits were compromised by the crash, or maybe the phone line was itself, but he made his way to the nearest 7-Eleven payphone and Jake answered his cell phone immediately.

"Jake! Holy fucking shit, are you at your pad on the coast? Where are you?"

"I'm heading your way. I got a call and I'm on my way. Are you okay?"

"Betsy! I can't find Betsy! She must've freaked out and taken off."

"Okay, she's probably fine. I'll know where to look for her. But are *you* okay?"

"Yeah, I'm fine, just sick about Betsy."

"It's okay, I bet anything she's fine."

"My God—this kid named Alex. Dude, I think you should sue. I bet you've got a lawsuit against the cops, or the guys that served the kid or somebody. I guess I'll head back to the house. Or maybe wait here? What's best? Can I go looking somewhere for Betsy and you can meet me at some…"

"Take it easy. I'm just glad to hear you're okay, just take it easy. Take deep breaths. So the car is still sticking out of the house?"

"Yeah."

"And your car is fine?"

"Yeah, it didn't get touched. I drove it down here to 7-Eleven to call you cause the phone... hold on—hold on."

"Why don't you call me back, I've got to catch an exit here soon."

Alex saw a shadow, followed it and sure enough it was Jake's old brown dog Betsy looking around the dumpster for something to eat. When Betsy saw Alex she immediately started whining and showing signs of stress. He gave her a few minutes of affection to calm her down a bit before he took her by the collar, went back to the phone and put her in a gentle headlock while calling Jake to give him the good news. Despite Jake's apparent earlier cool, he was very relieved about his dog, and then felt ready to start talking about immediate plans.

"Have you eaten anything lately?" he asked.

This was an ongoing joke of sorts. Anytime Alex was obviously depressed, Jake would ask two questions, one regarding food and the other regarding rest. It happened Alex was hungry, and so finally he replied, "I guess so."

"Well, how are the hot dogs looking inside that 7-Eleven store?"

"Not too good. From here I'm uh... not even sure they're up at the moment."

"I see…" Jake gave himself a long beat to consider possibilities. "But you do remember how to get Betsy in the car without hurting her hip."

"Yeah. Did it just the other day. But the house…"

"Well, you and Betsy are both stressed out by way of the house, and could probably use a little time away. And with a car sticking out of it, tow trucks on the way, and daylight hitting I doubt anyone is going to be so bold as to go looting in our neighborhood. I could probably use something or other to eat myself. I'm thinking fresh fruit. Which leaves your nearest 7-Eleven franchise out of the running."

Alex still wasn't sure what they were negotiating.

Jake continued: "Now the one on Santa Monica has fresh fruit, a microwave for frozen burritos if you're so inclined, and usually pretty darn good hot dogs."

"Okay…"

"The one on Sunset closest to you may not have fresh fruit, but it's where old Roy got punched in the face by that pimp, so it's kind of a sentimental spot, maybe worth stopping by to get some coffee after we eat, but…"

"Yeah?"

"Since you've got Betsy, and you probably want to hang out a while without her getting all antsy, I think we'll have to go to the one in Marina del Rey."

"Marina del Rey."

"Yes. Definitely. It's got everything the one on Santa Monica has, but it also has those beef flavored chewies Betsy likes, and that'll keep her busy while we chat. So…"

"Uh huh…"

"So!"

"Yeah?"

"Do you need directions?"

"Yeah, guess so."

"All right then. Let me know when you've got a pen."

A TIA for Gia

Gia had been working the night shift for about six weeks. She was always a little early, but one day she came in right at the time of her shift to find the register was alone in the back counted out for her, with a post-it note reading: "Gotta run, hope all is OK text me," with Andre's number scratched at the bottom. The last shift manager had left the money alone! What was going on?

Gia was already distracted because her boyfriend Elifèt had just moved to Boston to go to a better school to finish his business degree. They met in June at the University of Arizona, had a wonderful time together, but Elifèt had already decided to transfer before meeting Gia and felt the awkwardness of wanting to change his plans for a woman, but not wanting to act hastily, for fear of losing her respect. They had their plans well mapped, it was two years to finish, the visits and chats would be plentiful and the romance full of longing, then leading to marriage. But lately he had been distracted by his studies, and she wasn't sure how to read him over the phone yet, so excuses on his behalf were ominous to her—very unsettling indeed.

For Gia, the fear of introducing a Haitian fiancé to her strict Hindi parents was temporarily at bay, while the fear of losing Elifèt altogether and having no boyfriend at all at the end of semester was creeping up on her with surprising force. Meanwhile, what was going on with Andre? The previous shift manager texted her back a "Thnx," but no explanation. She sometimes saw Byron, the Store Manager on Thursday nights. Would he know what had happened? Byron often seemed to test his employees for loyalty, or there was at least something odd about his management style she couldn't put her finger on, but discomfort was gnawing at her and it looked as if it would be a fairly busy night. Friday was a holiday at University, and people were partying already so she wouldn't want to try to slip in a call to Elifèt before he would probably be asleep. Waking him was dodgy—might be he was sweet and reassuring, might be he was short and grumpy and she didn't think she wanted to chance it that night given how she had been feeling about him all week.

When Byron the Store Manager walked in, he already had a strange look about him that made Gia nervous, so she answered his questions with noticeable caution.

"Evening, Gia. How is the shift?"

"Fine, thank you."

"Nothing unusual?" and he was smiling right at her.

"Um, well not that I really..."

"It's all right, it's all right. Andre already told me what happened, don't worry, I'm just going back there to double-check the numbers. He had an emergency, it happens. Not that I want you to think it's cool to leave the register, nobody should ever do that, but as long as the numbers are all right we're all good."

"Okay, I'm sorry."

"No need, I'm just," and suddenly Byron paused curiously, then doubled over, took two big steps forward to barely grab hold of the counter to keep himself from falling. It was surprising to Gia that the glass of the counter didn't break considering how heavy he was.

"Sir? Byron, are you all right?"

Byron nodded, recovered his balance briefly, then staggered his vastly overweight body around to the back office and sat right down. Gia kept asking him if she should call the medics, but he kept sweating, convulsing, shaking his head and grimacing, "NO! Don't you call nobody. I bet you'd love that wouldn't you, if I were..." and then he let out a sound of pain; but he was so consistently clear in his insistence that he would be fine; Gia could only watch the front, help people out, go back and check briefly, then nervously pace outside the office.

He was back there for an hour before he finally started to feel well enough to stand. She got him some water, then he went and got himself a soda, looked at Gia and said, "Don't worry, I'll cover this before I go."

He was back there probably another forty-five minutes, breathing heavily but looking a lot more even when suddenly the love of Gia's life surprised her by walking right into the store. She actually saw him on the camera before she knew for sure it was Elifèt. She hopped over the counter to leap up again right into his strong arms and wrap her legs around his hips. That grin of his, that big, cartoonish grin was the most beautiful sight she thought she'd ever seen, as he explained that the school did not have all of the classes and opportunities this year that he expected, and he and his parents agreed that for the price it was better, the education he could get right there in Tucson, until perhaps those opportunities were to reemerge for him in Boston. This way Gia and Elifèt could talk about options, perhaps she might find something for her field in graphic design in Boston for the next semester, but he thought it was important that they be together while they made these decisions, because the distance could be very confusing at this stage of their relationship.

Byron now up and watching, knew something of this man and occasionally slapped his own right arm, which was still a little numb, while he insisted several times over that he could cover Gia's shift for her. She fought due to concern over Byron's health, but eventually the romance of Elifèt's surprise got the better of her and she reluctantly punched out, and even gave Byron a little hug before she left, saying with little tears in her eyes, "Just call me if you need me to come back."

Byron respected Gia and Andre as intelligent, dutiful, and highly ambitious employees who obviously wanted his position, who wouldn't? He knew he wasn't the sharpest guy who ever managed a store, and his health almost put his job up for grabs; but his perseverance was what set him apart. Gia called to check on him, probably just wanted to cover herself from any repercussions from corporate, but his night was made by the fact that this perseverance of his had given him some real dirt on two very ambitious junior employees in one night.

Seven Eleven on a Boat

The water is high and glimmering from where I stand. These Ballona Creek wetlands leading out into an unusually active stream of water are particularly muddy today while I'm finally getting Jake's boat ready after many days of thinking I might, and waiting for just such a day as this. Predictably, I brought nice shoes. My nicest shoes—brown Birkenstocks I just bought on sale at a Melrose shop for twenty dollars because Jake just had a lot of work for me, moving his and Tatiana's stuff into storage, and I have been buying any shoes at thrift stores that fit me for so long I can't even really say I have recognizable preferences where shoes are concerned. I take the Birkenstocks (or whatever they are) off, throw them and my wet socks in the direction of a nearby boulder and leave them figuring I'll find my way back here before dark.

Jake actually took me through the process of using this boat for an anticipated date, before he and Tatiana moved to their house on the coast back up in Oregon, and I decided to camp here on the property, near the house I was watching when the accident happened. I paid careful attention to his instructions about the boat with a date in mind, despite the fact that I have literally had about one date every three years for the past twelve years on average. And those dates, so isolated in time, would either lead into a relationship of three to twenty months, or let me wait another three years without in almost every case. And as I get older, I become less interested in winning arguments at bars, less interested in staking my claim as an actor, and increasingly interested in figuring out an explanation for my ongoing, banal solitude.

"Keep the faith," I've been told now and again. It's a lovely sentiment, and it obviously has to come from people who wish me well, but it comes from such a flawed understanding of my worldview. When did I have faith? Can someone please tell me one moment in my life when I've shown signs of that virtue—one definitive moment given my actions, or even a snapshot where it's showing on my face? As a child I played sports, and would continue to play hard even if my team was behind by many points, but is that really faith? Is the refusal to quit playing at life's tedious, oppressive, apparently lost or fixed game proof of anything other than the willingness to live another day? If so, in what shall I invest this faith? A business? A café with all the things I used to fancy? If I have shown signs of what I would call faith, it would be through my ongoing quests for a higher level of discipline in one of the many art forms I have explored; but I have doubts now, doubts that this will ever see me to feeling I have a head above water.

Perhaps you need evidence of this dedication. A few years ago, I maxed out credit cards totaling more than ten thousand dollars in order to produce a short film. I chose and treated a script with such ruthless care I probably lost most of my writer friends that year. The full-length script sprung from this same concept is, I believe, ready for production. Hardly a day goes by when I am not subjected to an internal showing of this unmade film, each scene is so clear and alive in my mind's eye.

But of the short film that actually exists in the world—I directed and played a secondary role in it, edited it painstakingly to the tune of another two grand I more or less owe to various friends including Jake. When that was finished, I felt the kind of satisfaction one rarely feels in this line of work; that once in a decade satisfaction of knowing it was as good as the thing could be. I had people over to Jake's place for a screening, at first only a half-dozen close friends (including Roy, a very successful writer now selling scripts almost every month it seems, for both independent and mainstream production). Quite a few of the guests were in tears by the end of it, so I hosted another screening opening the door to people in the movie industry I hardly knew, all of whom were so convincingly moved even I, of infinite skepticism, believed their applause. A handful of people stayed until three in the morning, despite early schedules, and I kept hearing the thing would have to be made, and we drank wine, life was outstanding and I felt my destiny sweeping me up at last.

But I didn't stop there. Of course those friends and acquaintances had lives, and of course they could only put a DVD on so many desks so I took detailed advice from Roy, and a friend of his, a big-name producer Roy got me in touch with. I sent copies out to various independent film investors from a list created with the aesthetic of my project in mind. I had meetings, and I came very close, and without any real stroke of bad luck I can put my finger on, faced a series of very reasonable explanations regarding why the full-length movie my short was meant to rocket into production was not quite timed for anything other than what is called an "option," and Roy suggested I wait instead of pocket the two grand it would have rendered.

So this little rowboat—this boat, on which I sit—this is what it all comes down to. This two-dollar cigar and forty ounce, skunky smelling fucking beer, this is where it's all led me. Jake, for Christ's sake, where in the hell do you get your faith in me? I'm going to take a woman on this boat, a woman? You leave me in charge of your house, a car goes crashing through it. You lend me money while I'm acting like a maniac in order to fail as a filmmaker, showing no signs of concern on the return or my lack of income. Every time you hear that I am about to ask some lady out and it falls through, you have words to pull my head out of the sand and encourage me to keep looking.

But finally the meaning is clear, the meaning of all of this, at least for now, and it's good I'm on your boat, Jake. I have never had an expensive cigar, so this cheap one makes no difference; and I have certainly dealt with my share of hangovers, so never let's mind the quality of the beer for the moment. It's this boat—this boat and something you said about your sailing trip to Hawaii that says it all. You threw something over. I don't remember what—a book, or a letter or something, you threw it over, and told me that it became the most purging discard of your life. Something about watching it sink—something about leaving it behind. All of these things in my past I have successfully surveyed as meaningless, all had one item at the very center, one very flawed item that if I can somehow bring myself to leave behind will purge, and renew my life for today.

I finish the cigar and throw the butt off to the right, aim this boat at the island where I was meant to have a picnic. The water hits my fingers and I worry it's shallow; my face hits the water and I wonder if I'll drown, but then I am under. Then I'm swimming. I look back only to be sure Jake's boat is washing up on the island now behind me, then I'm swimming and swimming more. I see beavers to my right. On a grassy area to my left and up ahead a good swim I see a homeless man who looks familiar but so worn, so very worn I hardly think to wonder if it's him. He's curious for all of twenty seconds why anyone is swimming this time of year until I get closer and he sees my long blond hair, then he starts squinting: "Hey rich kid! Is that you?"

I'm out of breath but manage a broken up sentence: "Who the...fuck you calling...rich kid, Aaron! Where are the rest of the guys?"

"Campground! I thought that was you. Kid Seven Eleven! We've been calling you 'Seven Eleven' this whole time cause we... the Indian's back in jail and we were just thinking about you."

I'm wading now, looking right at him. "I'll meet you there in about twenty minutes, just gotta get some clothes and a few bucks."

"All right, Seven Eleven. I'll see you there."

Swimming back downstream doesn't feel like backtracking. Changing direction is not the point I realize, and I might meet this guy for a beer or I might not.

***

I go back to the house, or campsite as it seems, and get some clothes out of the drawer in the garage where I keep a cycle of clean clothes, though most of my other stuff is in my car ready to move on to a better situation should it come up. I walk past the 7-Eleven where I was to meet Aaron because he's not there and a hot dog doesn't seem right for my hunger at this point. I sit down at the same little Mexican place again, as I can't seem to settle on an alternative no matter how I try. Inside there's a draft on my wet hair, but when I move to a sunny spot by the window, I find I can eat comfortably enough. I make my way back to those muddy shoes, then find the walk is a lot further through the bog than it seemed when I was alternating between rowing in still water and riding along with moving water; and finally I see the island where I left the boat and I'm glad it's still there.

I strip down to boxers and take yet another swim to the boat. I find the rest of my beer, the other cigar of a two pack, the lighter, and the cup I foolishly felt the need to poor soda into (soda I would immediately toss outside), in order to protect myself from a twenty-something year old cashier suspecting me of using the cup as I would—for drinking alcohol in public.

I look out at the shimmering water and hear my own voice saying, "It's a beautiful day," as I prop my feet on the rim of the boat and lean my head back on a rock. I smoke, drink right from the bottle, and realize that just now I sounded timid and uncertain to my own ear, so I say it again like I mean it, then a bit louder, and louder again, until there's an echo slapping back at me from the wood of the boat, then the water itself, all in celebration of something I do very much believe: "It's a beautiful day!"

Princess 7

Once there was a beautiful young princess named 7. She had been alone for most of her short life until married, lonely yet unaware of the implications of her solitude, and her sobbing mother who would only sometimes visit her in the basement and dress her strangely curved, yet elegant body in bridal clothes before dashing back upstairs at the thunderous command of 7's father, who 7 had never seen.

Down there for endless hours with nothing but a lantern and a mirror, she too would practice dressing herself in various combinations of the few outfits she had, though her bridal clothes were always taken back upstairs by Mother. She knew not how many days or months had passed when she was finally told of her wedding to be. When her half-brothers came down to tell her, they had very strange looks on their faces, and spoke cryptically of the wedding plans. Last she remembered of the basement they were telling her she wasn't a proper number, and that Father never loved her or would love her anyway, and they were penetrating her with drills, and spraying her with a bright red color, to disguise the very subtle, slightly fairer tone of her skin, compared with her half-brothers and her father. The three half-brothers assured her that *now* she would be able to satisfy a husband, now she had the proper color and fixtures, but

if she spoke of the ritual they had performed
on her to anyone, Father would certainly have
her killed rather than married.

7 was in denial throughout the ceremony.
Surely this was not the man Mother had been
talking about. He was a collection of shapes,
not one shape, and they told her that in the
modern world, in the country where she would
be living, numbers were spelled out in letters,
rather than pure; and they would have a
rectangle together above the city, and from the
moment the man leading the ceremony pressed
her body to his, she felt the end of all her fear
and excitement about the marriage, realizing
Eleven, a number who was actually a word,
would always be behind her, around her, and
inside of her on display.

Resigning herself to this life each morning
when she wakes up has slowly become a more
comfortable routine over the years. As the cars
that pulled up to the lot below changed from
steel to plastic, so has her previously inflexible
idea of what it meant to be a number changed
as per the necessity of her circumstances. She
has accepted that she as a number 7 does not
fit in this world. She had to tell herself that the
shape of her, on its own, has no human
purpose, and for this reason she could not
carry on with her dreams of anything different.
Placed against the word "Eleven," together they
can sell candy and cigarettes, and though
sometimes the thoughts of life on a house, as
part of an address with pure numbers like

herself, sometimes these thoughts do entertain her very stationary existence, she has grown wiser, or at least numb enough to accept that probably those fantasies are not all she imagined they might be after all; and anyway, there are many numbers who were deformed by the machines of their creation, therefore destroyed; and still others who survived yet never had the opportunity to know as many as these two different places she remembers— namely her parents' basement and the parking lot before her.

Occasionally she drifts so far away that she's nearly asleep yet sees everything; and she smells the smoke of a cigarette burning in the parking lot and she can't even feel the insipid presence of her hovering husband; and she dreams of a huge earthquake hitting the city; an earthquake so big it takes down houses and bridges, and surely this would be enough to shatter the fragile bond holding her to the sign; and she pictures the various arrangements in which their broken pieces might hit the ground as a splatter of plexiglass and thin aluminum— neither of them could be recognized but then neither again would they be bound to one another. And she sleeps easier on those evenings when she can see the picture clearly; or at least easier than when she was young and full of hope.

The Stoned and Angry Vegan

Kalob was throwing up and telling me it tasted like rubber bands; his 17-month-old sister was crying to be changed. I got things under control enough to call Tico back. Tico, the stoned and angry vegan.

Normally I wouldn't have bothered until Kalob was all better, but I had worn my brakes down on the truck, so the rotors had to be replaced and Tico was finally good for the money he owed on last month's order of Kombucha, plus a steady supply of chicken and goose eggs, so this next deal had to be made while he still had the money.

The good news was I had already convinced him I couldn't bring these things to him anymore. Bringing things to him meant either awkwardly and insistently deflecting his many attempts to inflict vapor hits of high-grade homegrown weed, or taking those hits and paying the price. It was so stressful turning hits down to hear him say, "Come on, no excuses," and tell me brusquely how I've changed while feeding me all kinds of hard-edged yet roundabout logic regarding what those hits would actually do to help me raise my kids and fix my car, but then if I took that shy hit, immediately he might start to feel like he could negotiate the numbers down where the agreed upon price of my latest batches of goods he would otherwise pay a set price for was concerned.

What I said was the errands I had along the way were too many to allow me to guarantee the preserved quality of the organic products I would deliver, and that with the kids in my life that would always be the case, at least in the foreseeable future. But since I wasn't at the Country Day School, where I have been teaching Agriculture and Environmental Politics, and keeping a certain amount of eggs and mushrooms in the school's refrigerator that much closer to town than my own farm, I knew this would lead to an abrasive conversation with Tico, even if he did end up coming to my farmland and giving me the money he already bloody well owed me.

Sure enough, he was quick to the point: "Awwww... fuck! You're gonna make me drive all the way out there? Think of the carbon man, what are you doing? It's bad enough going to the school, but ten miles out of fucking town? We're back to hurting the earth again, man, and that just blows my whole vibe about the deal!"

"Tico, look—my kids are both sleeping and they need this nap."

"But think of what your kids will grow up to! You've gotta figure this out soon, man, you can't keep expecting me to come all the way out there in my car, man, it's the laws of nature. You need a centralized fridge, like 7-Eleven, you've gotta figure out how to beat the system at its own game, and soon."

He had never come out to my farm, except once, the first and last time I let him try the Kombucha for the price of a little bit of his bud. I still had that bud, and my wife Anne has been using the word *boundaries* at every single mention of Tico's name since she met him; so I had better have cash to show for his visit if he did finally break down and drive out here, that's all I could think while he went on:

"It's our community responsibility, man! It's *our* responsibility as humans to find community solutions to social injustice. Or the corporations, man, those fucking scumbags are always gonna have the upper hand. Think about it. You've got to put together a subterranean revolutionary trade route on a local level first, then 7-Eleven is gonna have no choice but to give you a good rate for your goods, man. It's all they know is numbers, and the numbers will be working for me, for you, and even for fucking, Joe fucking Blowjob Yuppie man, all of us man. Everybody is gonna want your shit when they feel the spiritual righteousness of it, but you've gotta get that central fridge, or get me a key to the school, or sell to 7-Eleven or something, or the corporations will just keep squeezing our balls! Don't you understand— they've still GOT YOU BY THE BALLS, MAN?"

The problem is, see the problem is, <u>you're</u> the one squeezing my balls. You maniacal fuck, I *can't get a word in, and while I wait to give you directions and meet you probably three miles in your direction to lead you here, rather than take the chance you'll call screaming at me lost on some other poor fucker's farm because you can't get it together to write anything down; while I wait for this distinct pleasure of describing roads to you, together we are caught in a lost land between the fairytale Eden of some mushroom trip you never quite came down from in 1972, and a paranoid survivalist nightmare you're waking up to whenever you have another flashback; a nightmare days away from a world where paper money is no longer valued by those apocalyptic zombies tearing down your door to take your pot and my green-tea kombucha; but for some reason if you flash memorabilia printed gold coins in front of these same desperate zombie faces, who were minutes from tearing off your head and raping your brains before feeding on them, for some odd reason only gold will be respected in this final holocaust; only gold will recreate human understanding amidst the chaos and unfathomable violence following the collapse of the dollar; only with gold will humans and zombies be able to go back to negotiating as sensible capitalists with a mutual respect for fair trade, so to see them off saying "Thank you very much kind sirs. It's been a pleasure not feeding you with my flesh and internal organs, and I hope these gold coins and marijuana will see you to a well-deserved day of plunder; but not here, you shall not plunder here today, for I am a man who thought ahead. I am a man who*

*thought far enough ahead to spend my
disability checks on bottled water and precious
fucking coins!"*

I wanted to say all this, but I thought it instead
and said, "I've gotta go. Someone's crying again,
call me later, Tico—yeah...yeah—no really, I'm
serious, I really am hanging up now."

Too Nice

*(Story inspired by Cort Fritz; dedicated to Sa
Bum Nim Daniel Steven DiVito, 1942-2012)*

"You're too nice," Sensei smiled. "With most
students I talk to, I have to remind them what
martial arts is about, and that they shouldn't
use it to bully the bullies, but with you, you
take too much, and from what I'm hearing, it
might be time for you to stand your ground."

Jeremy had been telling him about an older kid
named Andrew who pushed him around a little,
to which Jeremy walked away; choked up, but
sure at least he hadn't broken his own code, by
attacking someone who hadn't really meant to
harm him, not really. Pushing was just a way of
showing you're bigger, and so until he threw a
punch he figured it wasn't a real attack. But his
instructor, Mr. White, had seen Jeremy work all
the way through his system to red belt, and felt
he knew Jeremy well enough to counsel him
thusly: "It's not a matter of whether or not you
can," and Mr. White smiled. "You can handle
grown men, you can do more than you realize.
If you've had enough of this guy, it might be
time for you to show him you've had enough.
Take care of business, wait and see if he's going
to get back up to come after you, and then deal
with that if you have to." And then Jeremy
heard something he never thought Mr. White
would say, especially not with the smile he was

wearing: "If you have to kick his ass, just kick his ass, Jeremy."

Jeremy was confused. Something felt off, but he kept it in the back of his head since it had been a great work-out, and it was a good half-hour at least before his mom would pick him up at the 7-Eleven down the street. There he would take the five dollars he was meant to spend on a hamburger, and buy that Big Gulp he'd been thinking about the entire second half of the third class he'd been involved in that night. He taught the first, assisted in the second and trained really hard in the advanced class for the third hour. He could already feel the burn of the soda down his throat, and then the rest of the money would be plenty to keep him busy on Q-Bert, even if mom was super-late.

He walked in the door in the best mood, the endorphins rushing enthusiastically through his brain, when suddenly his heart sank: Andrew was at the video game, smacking and body-bumping it, just on the edge of a tilt, with the confidence only older kids with much experience have when they play. He thought briefly about walking out and getting the burger after all, but then he thought of Mr. White's words and came up with another plan: he would fight him; he would kick Andrew's ass.

He worked it through in his head: he would put a quarter down on the video game. Andrew would notice him there, call him names like

"Scrub," and try to push him, at which point Jeremy would put a block together with a low kick, followed by a right cross to the guy's nose; then he'd use the surprise as an opportunity to open up on him. This had worked for him against a huge bully, couple of years into his training.

Or, if Andrew tried to steal his quarter he would just unload on him. His Sensei said it was okay, after all, and he was a lot more pissed at Andrew than he realized. Jeremy paid for the soda, pocketed the majority of the change but took one quarter to the game and smacked it down with all that pent up anger from previous encounters. Andrew looked over and said, "Hey Jeremy, what's up?"

This he hadn't expected. Andrew was in that rare friendly mood, like when out of nowhere he had given Jeremy his extra chicken nuggets at lunch. No friends around; that was the difference.

Andrew played another couple of rounds but still had a backload of guys left. "Shit, I gotta go," he said. "Could you play the rest of this out for me?"

Jeremy didn't say anything but took over when Andrew left. He knew Andrew better than to think the problem was over. His fighting strategy was still in place, and the next time, whenever, wherever it happened, the next time Andrew pulled any bullshit, even if there were enough big kid friends around to have to run away after doing it, the next time Jeremy would do as he had planned, and kick Andrew's ass without mercy. But the main thing that evening was that the 7-Eleven was still his, he was tearing it up at Q-Bert while saving his dinner money by playing Andrew's game; and a Big Gulp mix of various sodas had never tasted so good in Jeremy's life.

Seven Eleven Forgotten

1.

Once he was back to fairly steady work through temp agencies in Glendale, Alex again began to drink so regularly when he was at home that his occasional binge weekends out of town were growing excessive, as if to make a deliberate distinction between his working life and his short vacations. On one trip to Oregon, for example, he kept it relatively moderate when around his friends on the coast, Jake and Tatiana, but then went out on his own, staying mostly at bars around his little hole in the wall motel in Portland. He would lose track of his surroundings, and forget sometimes exactly what had happened the night before, such as had he joined another table for a drink or two, or actually sat by himself the entire night? He found such nights to be especially enchanting while taking his starter drinks the next day, because it gave him something to think on, and maybe look for clues about as he got himself to feeling regular by light lunch and beer at perhaps one of the same spots. When Alex offhandedly described some of these experiences aloud to Jake, he did notice some hints of concern.

Another longtime friend named Roy had a book signing, and came through town that Sunday, which convinced Alex to extend his trip by two days, allowing for a night out with these two older friends. Alex saw Roy as something of a mirror to his own hopeful future because of his success as a writer. On many occasions Alex would base life decisions on little bits of advise he managed to catch from Roy along the way, though he didn't look at him as a role model per se. Roy's bombastic methods in getting the attention of a publisher and eventually selling scripts to Hollywood, along with his ways with women, especially this in fact, kept most of Roy's methods themselves decidedly out of reach to the more introverted Alex. "Don't try that at home," was what he often thought when he saw Roy approaching an entire booth full of models or some such thing. When Alex did try that at home, so to speak, it was most often a reinforcement of Alex's original theory.

Alex had gotten from L.A. to Portland using the train, so the changes in schedule were all perfectly simple since his work was temp agency derived. Alex hadn't seen them since just after the crash at Jake's house. For the purposes of entertaining the group by means of self-denigration, he became candid about some of the binges he took during get away trips. Alex said he was researching a new script. Realizing he was in the company of another writer, Roy, he quickly mentioned that it had something to do with an isolated character that believed that staying in dive motels for the rest

of his life would make him sufficiently happy
for the duration of his ambulatory existence.
This they found charming at first, but as Alex
went on he compared this situation to his own,
and also said he intended to get his passport
back in order and go to just such a dive in
Moscow for his next trip.

Suddenly Alex had the table's undivided
attention, to where he wasn't entirely sure he
was entertaining Roy, Trenton (a friend of Roy's
who came up to Portland specifically for the
book-signing), and Jake anymore as much as
being quizzed about the relationship between
his script and his actual world-view. Jake knew
that Alex rarely dated, but people also seemed
very interested in whether or not he had been
with a lady anytime recently; further, did he
have a plan of action for such to occur
sometime soon? He managed to keep everyone
laughing, but later it occurred to him to
wonder—he had known two of these people for
long enough that they couldn't possibly be
questioning his sexual makeup; could they?
Considering the usually festive atmosphere
among this clan, the questions about his dating
life seemed a little off topic and direct.

Roy cracked a joke or two of false insinuation
about Trenton preferring men, who took this
gracefully, and this blanketed the tension Alex
felt. But the air of the conversation continued
to show subtle signs of very real concern about
Alex's well-being in general. Still Alex managed

to crack everyone up pretty regularly, and only once or twice more experienced alienation.

By the time the trip was over, Alex returned to Los Angeles with another of many ongoing inside jokes with Jake. The character in Alex's script would have lost his mind at the time of arriving at the Moscow motel. Alex didn't see any flaw in the idea that he was going to Moscow to research a motel and surrounding area, in order to set up his character's final days, yet when they were on their way to 7-Eleven the next morning, Alex seemed puzzled when Jake said, "And how does your researching this character's trip seem any more sane than the character taking the trip himself?"

When Alex caught on, they had a good laugh at that, and for several weeks on the phone, if Alex had been feeling particularly out of sorts, he might say something like, "Well, I have to admit I've been thinking *real hard* about renewing that passport lately."

"So, what are we talking here—you've got the paperwork, but you haven't filled it out, or you've filled it out but haven't sent it in, or *exactly* how far along in that process are we?"

"No no, just looking at the application on the internet. Checking out the process is all."

"All right then. You just let me know if you get that thing printed up next week or what the deal is."

And they laughed, but then a few weeks went by without their chatting because Jake and Tatiana were in Buenos Aires for Tatiana's mom's funeral.

2.

Coming back from his Northwest trip Alex had a few job interviews for potential long-term placements. After drinking with such disregard for a few days in a row, he experienced something closer to hallucinations for a day or two following his return, including the day of these interviews. Each of the people who interviewed him took on shifting, yet striking resemblances to insects. There was a lady who was wearing red and black, with a round body and round features and she seemed so remarkably like a big, beady-eyed ladybug that Alex kept having to look away in order to focus on her questions.

Next a mousey lady with her hair tied back in a bow appeared and sounded like a mosquito, to where Alex was looking for some sign of her having a mechanical device to help her speak. Perhaps the refrigerator in the other room was buzzing in a way that interfered with his perceptions, but still it seemed to Alex she was actually buzzing as well as speaking. Her tendency throughout the interview was to downplay the job she was interviewing him for, and invite him to get involved with an internet marketing venture she was investing in. When Alex offered the slightest hint of skepticism regarding the security of such a venture leading to high pay, working from home, she buzzed furiously, "Bzzz, I'm gizzing people a zzzchance to earn what they're worthzzzzzz!"

A third interview was held by a round fellow
who seemed to Alex to be as much potato bug
as man, and this was the job he ended up going
with, though all three of the supervisors
offered him long-term work in the end.

3.

After only a week in his new position, Alex found the version of Glendale, California vacant of his long-time friends, Roy, Jake and Tatiana, a place that was generally lacking in vitality. He picked up an account at the video store and started to settle in when one day he was parked at the nearest 7-Eleven of all places, and he locked his keys in his car. He requested assistance from a Latino clique that seemed fairly well versed at getting into his car quickly, and in exchange he offered a few of the beers in his 12 pack. While they took a couple more beers than he meant for them to, a Glendale Police car pulled into the parking lot to investigate. It was a suspicious looking scene, to be fair, and so Alex was ready to answer any questions and be on his way. Next thing Alex was getting his arms checked for track marks, and had a female cop of stern demeanor looking at his pupils with a flashlight and reporting back to the other officer: "No, we're looking at pupils about two millimeters over average in direct light."

"How are they responding?" asked her male counterpart seriously, and he stepped back in front of him.

"Slowly, and still at least one point five millimeters too big when they do." The woman officer gave the flashlight back to the other officer, went back toward the car while the man kept staring right into Alex's eye. "That and your cotton mouth points at the use of illegal substances, probably stimulants. Have you ever done cocaine, or anything intravenous?"

"No," Alex was already a bit flabbergasted. He was mildly hung over, nothing more.

"Come on…" the officer said, as he quickly and impatiently rolled back Alex's black, long sleeved shirt on both sides.

But discovering nothing on his arms didn't satisfy either police officer. They decided to call for another car to take him in. Alex wondered why they needed another car to take him in, but sufficed it to say, "This is turning into a terrible evening."

At the station, he found himself in a small cell with only one other occupant—a raggedy looking Caucasian man who was on the phone for quite a while, thereby postponing Alex's first call. The man on the phone was already in a fight with his significant other when they put Alex in, and Alex actually found the man's delivery worth watching while he waited to use the same phone. The man was scathing in tone and expression: "No. No, that's not what I said. No, you're not listening again. Do you… Do you want to listen to me for just one minute?"

Alex considered calling his current roommate, a med student in his early 30s, but thought better of it since the guy also owned the house.

He wondered how many of Jake's friends were in Los Angeles, or if indeed he might still have a couple in Glendale.

Meanwhile the man on the phone looked for a word in edgewise versus a girlfriend or wife on the other line: "No, honey I didn't get drunk at the park again. You're gonna love this. Honey, I'm in jaaailllll—get it? So how do you like that? Yeah, jail. Not for getting drunk in the park. I said not for getting drunk in the park."

Apparently this man had warrants based on traffic, insurance and other tickets unpaid. But as Alex drifted away from the conversation he thought he saw a policeman with an abnormally hairy face down the hall passing out a memo to another officer, who seemed a little bit too short to be in uniform.

When they led him downstairs to the lab for drug testing, he assumed a more confrontational demeanor. For the downstairs demands of urine and such, they had many opportunities to take handcuffs off, speak to him casually, always insinuating that he had to be on *something*, and Alex's patience for those tactics was wearing thin, especially once he learned that they were leaning toward keeping him until the drug results came in. Since their techs were going home shortly, that would mean spending the weekend in jail at least.

He ended up in a room by himself about the size of a walk-in closet. On all sides the walls were white cement blocks the size of those at the handball court near his house. Centered before him was what he assumed was a two-way mirror—a four by six-foot surface displaying a remarkably disheveled picture of Alex. He was wondering what was meant by the term "two-way mirror," since only one side of it acts as a reflector, when the hairy officer he caught a glimpse of upstairs walked in. The man was stranger looking than Alex had even thought, or allowed himself to visually interpret. He was hairy on every part of his face and hands, but not like an ordinary monkey, because the black hairs were extremely thin and long. His eyes were dark, but encoded by years of experience in his field; or possibly years of training in the aggressive objectivity of his district's laws and protocol. Over a short period of time Alex learned that there was absolutely nothing about the man Alex could read by looking past the tangled hair to gaze directly into his eyes. He kept gazing while they spoke, at first with open irritation, then eventually real psychotic anger, seething from constant exposure to this unit's act of injustice against him, and the shamelessness of every State servant involved.

The beastly officer was nearly whispering, "I have to hand it to you, you do stick to your story."

"I've told you, not a story."

At this the cop took off his cap, revealing a vacancy of hair at the very top of his head Alex did not see coming. It seemed he removed his cap to give Alex the impression he was finally leveling with Alex, as he spoke just slightly more casually: "I know, that's the impressive part, is how you stick to it, despite the fact that every one of us knows you're on drugs. Most people would have let up by now and confessed it, because it's so very obvious."

"I don't know how many different ways to tell you, the drug test will do my talking for me! There's nothing else to do but wait for the proof, and I understand you think you have reason for suspecting me, but I'm simply asking you to please imagine yourself in my shoes. Or even in your own shoes. Let's just say that in the process of supposedly doing your job, you've been keeping me here all this time unnecessarily, and you come to learn this from clean test results. If I've had to stay here the weekend, would that not bother you in the least?"

"My job is to uphold the law, and to do so according to what I see. I see a guy on either speed or coke. As for putting myself in your shoes, I can't picture myself as a drug user, so I can't really put myself in your shoes, Mr. Aronovich. Pupils of people who aren't under the influence of stimulants do not look the way yours do. If you are clean, and your pupils are doing this, you ought to go to a doctor and get a note you can carry around stating that, because what I'm looking at right now are not normal looking eyes."

The insinuation didn't even end when they were driving him back to his car. Alex asked, almost desperately what they suggested he do to avoid this happening to him again in the future, to which someone up front replied, "Well, I guess the best thing would be to uhh, I don't know... I guess to do what you say you're doing, and stay away from drugs, and people who use drugs."

4.

It turned out Trenton, the guy Alex met in Oregon through Roy and Jake, was the last contact Jake had in Glendale; it also turned out Trenton had a spare room. Alex moved in quickly and found Trenton's company briefly enjoyable, after that at least justifiable given the urgency Alex somehow felt to change addresses. The hairy cop had said, "You know if anything turns up in this test we're going to take you back in, right?" Alex had no fear of the results of the drug test, but plenty of fear of the criminal justice system as he had experienced it, so this reactionary change in residence was just a decision like many he made before it, and he took a strange comfort in leaving no forwarding address with the med student.

So it was at this new address where his mom Theresa came and saw him, and insisted on getting him a new bed. The place was bare because he had only just moved into his last room and still had a few things back there, so the bright sparkly new bed in what was otherwise just a bachelor's barren abode of functionality, was indeed shining in comparison to its surroundings. It was literally shining, as new brass beds will.

One night Trenton turned down a friend of his for a night out to catch drinks, and instead Alex and Trenton sat and watched a movie, drinking beer for long enough so that Trenton found the opportunity to admit how he'd lost his last roommate, Chamberlin: "That dude was just sort of a stick in the mud, I didn't have anything against him. One night our mutual buddy had a birthday and we decided you know, arbitrarily to make a big deal of it and someone wanted to get a stripper. And this guy Chamberlin, white dude that thinks he's a rapper or a B-boy or whatever, you know the type, he didn't even feel you know, comfortable with it so at first I was going to let it go, but he had to bring it up again, what a bad idea he thought it was, and so I grab the phone book to be a dick, saying, 'Well I'll just call a few numbers,' and he just jumped at me and we started fighting."

"Jesus," Alex grumbled and squinted.

"Yeah—and you know how it is, he swore he won, I swore I did and so now we can't even get through a TV show without getting all shitty about it, so that's why he moved out."

5.

Annabelle was seven years older than Alex, but kept herself looking fairly young and fashionable, as informed by European style. She was 5'3", with short dark hair. They met at a bar through mutual friends, then much later in the evening at Denny's she announced to the table that things had been bleak at the bars that evening, then turned to Alex and said "I've just been watching you the whole night," and Alex was younger then, wide-eyed, always had a hard time taking compliments so he said, "You're very forward." All she said to that was, "I'm thirty-five."

Here it was now five years after he'd had anything to do with her at all, yet so much happened between them the short time they knew each other, it was like looking back on a short film. Very quickly after meeting, Ana rented an apartment for the two of them, that Alex would have to clear out of for a couple days whenever her boyfriend from Alabama, Shawn, was visiting. Soon Shawn presented the idea of moving to California to be with Ana, who was forthright about telling this to Alex. She stopped sleeping with Alex, but kept sort of residing there with him just after that first visit from Shawn. Then she came home very early one morning, crawled into bed with Alex "one last time," since Shawn was finally committed to moving. She said it made it kind of hot in the "one last time" sense of the experience, and it was that, it was hot. But not much between them since, maybe a drunken New Year's call where she was bored enough to pick up.

Out of the blue she called him at Trenton's as casually as she might sound. She said she got the number from Jake, and that Oregon number added up to about where he would have been the last New Year he had the brilliant idea of calling her and God only knows who else.

Alex agreed to meet in an hour at the Silver Spoon, a diner in Glendale. He was driving several blocks, and surveying what he could hardly refer to as a relationship, given Shawn's looming long-term status with her. Alex even went out with the two of them during one of Shawn's visits, so Ana could enjoy the pleasure of cornering Alex for a tongue kiss while Shawn was in the restroom and this sort of thing. Then suddenly she was moving out, claiming that she was getting confused and tangled up; and at one point they got in an argument that had Alex saying things to Ana like, "Has it ever occurred to you that it's a person you moved in with? Did you ever fucking think about that?" Ana remained poised throughout that argument and most everything between them. That she was so poised, so much of the time was a point of serious aggravation and attraction for Alex, and if he hadn't quickly gotten caught up in another affair he probably would have attempted to persist through that aloof quality to something deeper if it were there. Many times Alex wondered what would have happened if he had outwardly interfered with her long-term boyfriend, such as by making a scene in front of him. Instead, once Ana and Shawn moved in together, to another place, Alex found himself in awkward contemplation of the little bit of mail Ana was getting after two months in the little apartment where she had left Alex to writhe, pace, attempt to write her off and obsess over her ad nauseam—again, until there was another woman to fill the void of Alex's unscrupulous affections.

Even as Alex came to see the Silver Spoon logo he felt he had no real opinion about what they were to each other, more like six years later he was thinking. What was the meaning of this appointment? Why would she suddenly want to meet up? Was it vanity? Some detail that protected a small piece of Alex's dignity from the chaotic mess of their attempt to co-exist; something she had in the back of her head on some list, to revoke from him in retrospect? Once she might have shown signs of having gotten a little hurt when he commented lustfully on one of her friend's outfits with all the blundering ignorance of a twenty something year old rookie; but the very nature of their relationship was surrounded by honest comments about their sexual environment, and anyway, when push came to shove between the two of them, she never let on in the least, if her feelings had ever grown beyond those of a passing fancy. If there was anything more to it, she hadn't given him much of a hint; in fact quite a bit more than a hint to think there was almost nothing between them, especially looking back on it a bit older, and more carefully guarded a person as he was pulling into the diner parking lot.

Then it came, the odd sense of excitement walking through the door. Against all reason, all interest even, the apprehension took a back seat to his curiosity and perhaps something basic in him as a man that needed to think in terms of nesting, in spite of all his attempts at self-refinement since their miserable affair.

Alex's comfort with himself under the circumstances surprised him. He knew his social skills had improved immensely since they knew each other, but he didn't expect to carry on a conversation with Ana without feeling extremely awkward. He made her laugh about his ongoing disinterest in career, and at some point after there was food on the table Ana made her way in with a grand apology: "I was a flake back then. Really. That was a very flaky time in my life, and I'm sorry it caused you such grief."

Alex shook his head defensively, "I'm not here to sort anything out. I'm just glad to be—I'm just coming to remember that I have always found you easy to talk to."

"You too, Alex, you too. I told you about things in my past I literally didn't even tell Shawn, or my girlfriends back then."

Two things came to Alex's mind. One was a night she said she had been with an entire football team in her high school cheerleading days; the other was about a live in affair just previous to Alex's short stay with her, an affair with a young, middle-eastern terrorist. He thought for a moment over why these things from her past, and their past together still didn't entirely bother him, and again came to the conclusion that the part of him that was wired for nesting had no particular bounds—he was capable of starting a new perspective out of absolutely any sense of attraction. He was drifting off, dangerously far from the table, into the sort of mood he could not carry on a conversation in, so he quickly asked, "Are you still with Shawn?"

"Oh, no no no. I'm a free agent. I keep my hair short like this when I'm on the prowl," she smiled. Alex heard the slightest return of her Alabama accent, found it fetching, but quickly again started feeling hollow and even sick for the rest of the meal. He saw her as interesting, still very attractive, but couldn't get over how well she had kept it together in their split so long ago—how little it seemed to mean to her.

Just as easily as Alex was repulsed, the conversation shifted him out of the sick feeling in his stomach, when Ana complimented him: "From what I read of your writing back then even, I'm just surprised you're not already famous," and the next thing he knew he was inviting her over, introducing her briefly to Trenton while he grabbed some wine, splitting the bottle on that nice brass bed.

Ana got pretty flirty, and leered at him now and then whenever he started thinking fancifully about making a pass at her, and before long she asked about whom he had been seeing, and he said no one, no one for quite sometime, and she said, "Well, you know that's your choice, right? You know you could have anyone you wanted if you just..."

"If I what?" Alex asked pointedly, and that's when Ana finally just leaned in, and Alex kissed hesitantly back but before long they were touching tongues, and Alex went to get under her shirt and she said, "Later, not yet. I want you to know I really want it bad if we're getting together again," and something about that sounded familiar, something about it all seemed way too familiar, and as he left her napping, on his walk down to the 7-Eleven where he had been arrested before, he found the walk refreshing, and thought better of the whole thing; thought maybe he and Ana might actually be suited as platonic friends. With Jake out of town permanently, since the house by Bologna Creek was on the market, and with Alex having no inclination to reach out to any of the three or four plausible young ladies he worked with, helping old folks, it followed he could use a friend, and he didn't think he required much as a friend. They could even go out, she could help him meet other women since she was always outgoing, and it was as much as he could want from her after the strangeness of their first time around in each other's lives.

When he got to his room and opened the door, he felt an utterly involuntary grunt come out of his mouth, before he could even put together what he was looking at. Ana was naked, facing him, then it turned out she was sitting on top of Trenton who had his left hand wrapped around her torso, just under her breasts, and was rubbing between her legs with his right forefinger while she bounced up and down on him. Trenton was wearing most of his clothes, so only had time to hike his pants down it seemed, yet Ana was completely naked. Alex stood there while they continued in their sex-play as if he hadn't shown up, excepting that both Trenton and Ana were looking at Alex directly in the eyes. Alex was paralyzed for what seemed like about a dozen of Trenton's quick thrusts from beneath her petite, naked body, quivering with pleasure and empty of emotion at the sight of Alex's confusion, disgust, and borderline disbelief at what he was witnessing. As he stumbled backwards, he dropped the paper bag with the bottle of wine on the couch in the living room, and soon both Trenton and Ana reached outrageously vocal climaxes.

6.

Alex somehow got to a motel in Bakersfield. He did remember making a decision once he figured out which highway he was on. The wine bottle was open and available in his coffee cup holder along the way, and he had no trouble at all sorting out a room for himself once he got there. He did enjoy the unfamiliarity of the room and the surrounding area when he occasionally went out for refills and a bit of food. The TV almost always seemed hilarious, and whenever he found he wasn't cackling on a regular basis to look at it, he would take a bath. It seemed slightly poetic and fitting when he was suddenly on the phone with Jake, because Jake said he'd been trying him back in Glendale for a few days, and there were people worried, and Alex assured him that he was having the time of his life in a motel near the 7-Eleven they'd always talked about going to. The reason Jake already knew this was because a call on the phone card Jake had given him a couple years back showed a town on it, and the billing cycle had literally just gone through. "Really," Alex mused, "Who did I call?"

"Me."

Then Jake presented a convincing argument that Alex didn't have much of a plan, needed to stop drinking, and so he should check into a rehabilitation clinic back in Los Angeles after Jake came out and saw him. This sounded reasonable, and so Alex carried on with his festivities for another day while Jake made arrangements and found his way to Alex's motel. The plan was to get him to a clinic Jake had picked out. They spent the evening hanging out, and Jake found a surprisingly good time of drinking and relating old stories. They even got Roy on the phone so Alex could brag about heading to rehab the next day. All Roy said was, "So you beat me to it..." and then, "Well, write everything down, write everything down."

When Alex woke up, he found that Jake was still in the easy chair by the door, had probably only had an hour or two of sleep, but kept in good spirits about getting Alex to some help. He needed to get a couple of things from where he was staying, and although the thought of bumping into his roommate disturbed him, Alex felt it was important enough to get a couple of those things, such as the journal he was keeping and a favorite pen.

Instead of Trenton, Alex bumped into Trenton's ex-roommate, Chamberlin at the house. Chamberlin was Anglo, and of such similar build to Trenton that Alex confused the two, and walked past without a word thinking he might silently grab what he wanted and leave. Once Chamberlin identified himself as the previous resident, he was very outspoken about Trenton. Chamberlin's grasp of street culture may have ended as far as dialect, but he was nonetheless forthcoming with that dialect as if it were his only way of talking. Alex had no interest in conversation, but found himself thinking things he wanted to say while listening to Chamberlin go on, having apparently no idea that Alex's falling out with Trenton was at least as long-term as was Chamberlin's physical altercation over some petty disagreement about whether or not to invite strippers to some guy's birthday party.

Chamberlin stood at Alex's bedroom doorway, and preached: "I'm gonna tell you right now, do not trust this man you staying with."

Don't trust him. Okay, I'll try to keep that in mind.

"He makes like he's a rider, but he ain't no rider, I'm telling you brah, for your own good." Chamberlin's eyes widened even further to underline his point, "He makes like he's cool with you, but it'll be way more important for him to be cool with all his other boys once they come around."

Yeah, or perhaps some woman I might happen to leave in my bed for the twenty minutes it takes to walk to the store.

"How long you been staying here?"

"Umm, I don't know, just a couple weeks, I'm uhh...on my...way..."

"I definitely recommend you keep your options open, definitely, and I wouldn't be tellin' you this if I hadn't already been there done that, you know what I'm saying?"

I do. I do know what you're saying, now for the love of God, <u>please</u> stop fucking saying it.

"I'm telling you I used to hang with him real tight, yo. And I would still hang with him, I don't give a fuck I'll hang with you and I just met you, I'm down to hang with anyone, get some beers, go out and get some pussy, some weed, and I'm always cool like that and always have been."

Rehab—I'm going to rehab and I can't tell you how much better that sounds right now than what you're offering.

"But once Trenton gets a couple of his boys over…"

Or some horny acquaintance of mine…

"…he is way more down with his boys."

So you're saying he's not what you would call a 'rider'? Well, let me tell you something. If listening to your bullshit slang, you lanky, Orange County-born white rapper wannabe twit, if listening to you for one more fucking second is what it takes to be a 'rider,' buddy, I'm a whole lot closer to Trenton than I ever thought I could be. I know how you got into a fight. It had nothing to do with a stripper! He wanted to coax you into coming after him so he'd have a

*witnessed excuse to pummel the ever-living shit
out of you. Trenton walks in right now I'm
taking you down, holding you and begging
Trenton to forget the whole thing about Ana,
but please hold nothing back so I can say, "Yo,"
and let my arms sway back and forth a few
times so you can see how fucking stupid you
really look when you talk and talk and talk.*

Alex had his things and made to go scan the
bathroom, saying, "Excuse me."

"It's all good."

Chamberlin followed him to the bathroom and
stood in the doorway again. Alex felt that
maybe if he started the conversation it might
not be so unbearable: "So how long did you stay
here?"

"I was here on and off for a little while, good
little while but I'm telling you, bro, keep your
options open 'cause he acts like a rider but he
ain't no rider yo! I'm telling you!"

When Alex finally got out the door to get in
Jake's car, leaving his own in one of very few
long-term parking spots on the street in that
area, all he finally did say to Chamberlin was,
"Well, thanks I guess."

7.

After treatment, and as Alex kept up with the addiction program he started there, all kinds of historical dots started connecting as he listened to other people tell their stories of alcohol addiction. And Alex would even reach what he called epiphanies at these meetings so that for a few months the word "alcoholism," and the concept of an addiction as a disease settled in as a more logical explanation than he had expected, until it became something like a pet. This pet word, "alcoholic," would be there and ready to whisper simple answers in his ear; answers to what used to be some of life's most baffling and incessant questions.

On Thanksgiving Day he decided to go to the church where the program was holding an event. He caught sight of Trenton out of the corner of his eye, at a meeting after a great big dinner. Alex tried to dodge Trenton, but was eventually standing right in front of him as per Trenton's maneuvering as Alex headed for the exit. They hadn't spoken in sometime, and Alex had little reaction to Trenton's presence at first. Alex immediately put it together that he probably was headed toward Alex to offer an "amend" for the incident that, as far as Trenton could tell, led to Alex going to treatment.

But Trenton seemed to be talking down to him now that they were face to face, and Alex felt agitated instantly, a feeling that would only get worse as they exchanged words.

Trenton said, "I haven't seen you in these rooms before."

"I go to a small men's group—it's all I have time for," he lied. He had been to other groups, was still getting acclimated, but a quick out of the conversation was what Alex was after.

"Well, have you got a good sponsor?"

"I guess, yeah—not long have I been here."

"Well, if you want me to recommend someone...or if you want to change groups, I'm leading a good sized bunch of people—we don't dress the truth up very much, but we would take good care of you."

To Alex, this was absolutely astounding. Trenton seemed to be indirectly offering himself as a sponsor, or the person who would guide Alex through his steps to sobriety. Alex figured he couldn't have understood the situation correctly and said, "How long have you been coming to these groups?"

Trenton's smug condescension could no longer be mistaken. He smiled at one corner of his mouth and said, "Actually, I've been coming to meetings since I was seventeen, son. You met me during a very short relapse, and even though the situation wasn't ideal, I'm really glad that in some way my influence managed to get you to admit you have a problem."

Alex's stomach burned. He shook his head, almost watched Trenton turn away, but instead let go with everything he had in one solid punch to Trenton's abdomen. Trenton doubled over, but Alex wasn't satisfied. Realizing in that instance that he had in fact repressed anger over Trenton's exploitation of his loss of face to an ex-girlfriend, Alex grabbed Trenton's right ear with one hand, and his sweater with the other to slam him into an old fashioned metal radiator after about a six foot trip worth of momentum. Trenton fell to the floor from the impact, and the picture of him diddling and fucking Ana simultaneously flashed through Alex's head as he kicked down once, twice, and a third time at Trenton's neck before walking out of the church and getting in his car. A couple of people from the gathering started realizing what was happening and bent over to talk to Trenton, while a couple of others followed Alex out and started memorizing and reciting Alex's license plate number.

Alex turned on the radio and turned it up. He was driving away from the scene of what would doubtlessly be an utterly misrepresented crime of assault, while listening to James Brown's tune, "Revenge." It was ridiculous, but Alex felt freer than he had since he was drunk at the motel in Bakersfield.

They found out 7-Eleven was closed for renovations. The ultimate failure—for years they'd joked about going to that location so Jake could smoke out the window for the hour and a half or so it took to get there, giving Alex plenty of opportunity to ramble on about whatever he cared to. Now that Alex was getting ready to check into a facility, this 7-Eleven decided to shut down. A sense of significance disgusted Alex and he quickly shrugged it off learning from a pedestrian there was a liquor store closer to downtown.

It was at that liquor store where Jake picked up a piece of paper by the front doormat, tucked under the mat just enough that it wouldn't blow away. On one side of the 8½/11 page were three groups of boxes, long horizontal lines with short lines cutting them vertically into maybe twelve sections. One end of the stacked boxes was closed, the other opened so the lines were sticking out by a few centimeters. On the other side of the paper were just six handwritten words, "Even Big Goats Don't Answer Emails." Alex became very interested in the words and the figures while Jake went in to purchase the wine, because Alex didn't look like much.

Alex grabbed a back-road to the post office where his box had been for a few months. Why was he going there? What did it matter? Habit he supposed, for lack of a better plan, but in the PO box he found something he wasn't thinking about at all: his passport.

Alex blacked out the part where he was passing out slowly, telling Jake he was scared shitless to go to the treatment center, telling Jake over and over, "I'm tired—so tired," then later, "I'd rather die than go to rehab."

Along with the passport there was something in there for Trenton. He vaguely remembered letting him use the box number for some kind of software trial he was scamming for a second computer, and almost chucked it out the window when he suddenly saw Trenton driving away from where they once lived together. And Alex still had a key. He looked at the passport, fingered the key, and suddenly had a bigger rush of déjà vu than ever since he was a child, when those feelings were frequent and overwhelming.

"Tell me three things you like about yourself." The man was animated, speaking to a room full of coffee swigging and candy and cigarette trading grungy people in light blue scrubs. Someone said he chose treatment over jail only because of his family; he specifically wanted to see his daughter sooner than jail would have allowed. Another said she was good at seeing the humor in things. It got to Alex's turn and he said he thought he was very creative, "Oh three things, well I consider myself creative verbally, visually and intellectually," and it seemed an uncomfortable answer for the group therapist, and everyone in the room to hear at first, but then others followed suit and started talking about what areas of their lives they felt were

*creative, though some of these people sharing
weren't using the word to its actual definition;
for example Alex heard a man say, "You know I
feel like it's kind of creative the way I checked in
here, because I didn't let anybody I know see me
that way, and I just left a note and some money
for my roommate." The therapist's parting
words to send all these broken humans back to
their cots even included something about,
"Positive creativity."*

While Alex had willfully and fairly successfully
given up on a very strong tendency to view
coincidental phenomenon in a superstitious
way, he was unable to view this latest series of
events as pure coincidence. He had broken the
law in a State not long after losing all respect
for so-called criminal justice in that same
State—specifically by means of assaulting a
non-aggressive person he felt utterly justified
in assaulting—then he found his passport ready
to use in this box. Alex heard the phone ringing
as he was pinching Trenton's prepaid credit
card he knew was often left by the computer
when he was drunk, shopping late at night.
Everything seemed to fit so curiously in place
that he went to the phone to pick it up. He
heard an Indian accent: "Hello, may I please
speak to Trenton Tibbons?"

"This is."

"Yes, this is People's Bank. We just wanted to
remind you before Black Friday that the

spending limit on your credit or debit cards on any given day is three thousand dollars."

"Excuse me?"

"Just because we do have a lot of shoppers over this holiday weekend hit their limits, we wanted to let you know and that your cash limit, Mr. Tibbons, is going to be 500 dollars per day over the weekend, for prepaid gift cards or credit cards as well. Now, Mr. Tibbons."

"Yes?"

"May I ask would you be interested in a free trial for our new service called, 'Secure Travel...?'"

But Alex was already unhearing as he politely finished his conversation with the helpful representative of People's Bank; as he was unhearing of Chamberlin's voice as Chamberlin had moved back in but "Only temporarily, believe that 'cause like I already told you about Trenton, he is not trustworthy," and Chamberlin dug up some of Trenton's best scotch out of his room and the only thing that Alex kept thinking about besides how really good expensive scotch can be was the timing, the timing of his purchase, Trenton's work-day, and just how perfectly everything seemed to line up; and how strange it was, coming to this apartment to drop off a piece of mail and maybe a fun little note for Trenton right next to it.

He started toward Burbank airport, but his car broke down coming off the freeway, so he left the car there and was waiting at a bus stop with signs bragging of airport transportation, when he started to take notice of the guy who was sitting there under the awning. It was the man who had been on the phone at the jailhouse, speaking to his woman so derisively yet hilariously. Alex thought of reintroducing himself, thought better, then anonymously approached him once he realized he needed change for a five in order to pay the fare. The man was friendly enough in looking through his wallet, realized he was in the exact same predicament and assured Alex they'd be able to find someone to help once they boarded.

Well, they did get on the bus with the driver's blessing, got some change from a man who was standing with a crutch, due to a missing leg. He was a scruffy African- American man who mumbled a bit, then gave Alex something like three dollars worth of actual change for the five. When Alex suggested it wasn't the right amount, the one-legged man quickly punched Alex in the face. "I don't need to take that from you—I know this man," (he pointed with his chin at the man from the jailhouse who had gotten the right amount of change), "I know him, you know, but I don't have to take nothin' from you."

Alex sat down listlessly, just across from him. He asked his neighbor, a streetwise, stout black guy wearing crosses on a necklace and an earring, if in fact he had just been punched in the face by the little man sitting across, and his neighbor confirmed, and Alex kept staring at the little one legged man, and then engaged his neighbor in more discussion.

"Should I have hit him back?"

"No, I don't reckon that would've done no good."

"The day I've had, the month I've had, I'd just assume kill someone for that, but…"

"No I just think it's best the way you left it. Just mind your own business and keep to yourself is the best you can do."

The little man got up and hobbled to a seat closer to the front, talking to the driver, talking to others about football, or a celebrity trial.

Alex laughed to himself about the incident briefly, and how important things seem when there is any kind of shock involved, but then again he was suddenly very uncomfortable having casually mentioned the idea of killing a handicapped man on that bus. The same man was not looking in Alex's direction the many times Alex checked back. After fifteen minutes or so, enough people had left, including his neighbor, so that social tension left him and drowsiness was coming on. This mildly sleepy sensation became heavier without Alex noticing, until the sense of purpose he felt in lifting Trenton's gift card was ambiguous, and his plans to leave the country were also under suspicion. Perhaps Alex would first take a room right there at the airport, in hopes of sleeping away his doubts and restoring that wave of excitement he felt after tasting Trenton's hidden stash of scotch. It wasn't a moral question, Alex was wrestling with, it was a question regarding what Jake and Alex used to refer to as *the wave.* The wave was their word for the greater flow of life, that one might understand during a brilliant stroke of artistic heights, or from some heroic act of self-sacrifice, or in the blind pursuit of one's love; but regardless of the circumstances, the wave meant an experience without much in the way of second thoughts, and second thoughts now plagued Alex without question.

As he fell in and out of sleep, he finally lost interest in the debate, in favor of a sudden admiration for the trees of Burbank, California in late fall. There were ferns of sublime yellow and orange leaves, draping all the way to the ground. He was hypnotized, and dreaming he was tangled and artfully bound by the very light branches growing in through the slightly open window behind him; they tied him to his seat, and broke away from the tree to hold him so that he was caught there, unwillingly then resignedly missing the airport, watching the driver double back his route and then passing by the area where he left his little Toyota. He woke up mid-dream, then fell asleep again to the same dream, only this time he was on the bus while it passed his Toyota getting stripped for parts by a negotiating team of homeless people and corrupt police officers.

He woke up at the airport and unbound by foliage he had the liberty of getting out, asking an agent if there were any standby tickets available to Moscow; and the real matter of enjoyment for him wasn't in using Trenton's gift card without having to answer any questions about a signature or how he obtained it, but the way the lady seemed so very shocked about where he was going, and the fact that he was so flexible in his requirements for the trip. Would he prefer to get a Visa in New York, since the immediate flight would be leaving too soon to be sure he had time for the paperwork, and Alex would answer with words like "Sure," or "Fine," and since he was out of practice with liquor, he got drunk enough at the airport bar that the pilot and everyone seemed to be watching him pretty suspiciously getting on the plane. Once he had a good sleep, napped on and off in New York, after he prepared some forms for customs, he found that the Russian and American stewardesses and stewards and nearby passengers on the plane were very nice to him. Since years of playing with the idea in his mind, he was headed for the furthest reaches, as far away as that impulse in him commanded. He took long breaths, and was offered free drinks, and learned that good Russian vodka has almost no taste, and that the U.S. embassy was always looking for English speaking Americans. One of the jolly old Russian men he made friends with assured him with such confidence that he could easily pick up his Russian as he went; and anyway, Alex wasn't all that concerned because he had just enough room on his own credit cards not to think too hard, not to think too hard about anything, and soon enough he was drifting into yet another welcome nap.

When little Alex woke up the air was fresh, like it never is in L.A. and at three years old he really wouldn't understand such things, but there was something absolutely magical in the air that morning. He went straight out the door of his room, only pushed over a couple of plastic toys along the way and there wasn't much noise so his mom and dad stayed in bed as he made his way out the big front door to the front yard. And he knew in his heart exactly how important the air was, and how important it was that he must make his way out of the gate, and he was right! It wasn't latched the way it sometimes would be to keep him from getting out, and that quickly he was marching down the sidewalk with no doubt whatsoever, no doubt in his heart or mind, no fear or anything but that feeling one has at the beginning of true adventure, the kind of feeling explorers had to carry with them to continue traveling through adversity few humans ever know.

The sights on the street were more colorful and fascinating than they had ever been as viewed from a stroller, or holding hands with one of his parents. A car passed, and then another, and there was still nothing to fear!

He reached his destination and found that things inside were more complicated, but also bright and inviting. The man he might have seen before said, "Where are your parents?" and he got on the phone and started talking again, but Alex found the banana he had come for and left the belt of his little robe in trade.

And as his mom came rushing in he was already walking out the exit door and flapping in the wind for lack of a belt, and the storekeeper was right behind Alex as his mom and the storekeeper quickly determined what had happened and laughed, but the spell was not broken walking back home with his mom. He kept the banana and maybe his mom had the belt after all, didn't understand, didn't understand that he'd left it there for the storekeeper, but which store was it?

Out of this dream that almost miraculously revitalized a real childhood memory, he awoke wanting desperately to know the name of the store. He was already crying, and mouthed the words, almost said it out loud as he woke: "What was it called? I can't remember what it was called."

And for a while again he didn't drink at all, just stared out the window into the darkness and the air and felt completely without a destination or returning point.

8.

Alex did have some trouble at customs because he misunderstood a bit of the paperwork, but when he said he had a lead on a job at the U.S. Embassy and would update to a work Visa as soon as he could, they were not as particular and soon let him through. He immediately went shopping but didn't buy much other than some thermals and wool socks; he figured his winter clothes from the Northwest of the United States would at least be helpful for survival against the Russian winter. Next he found his way to a hostel that did accept the pay card he took from Trenton's desk, and paid for a two-week stay.

***

Soon he had a go-to bar to be bored with, a place called *Tupik*. It was the first bar he tried after settling in and they served sausage and, as the cute British couple next door to his room assured him, enforced no drink minimum, which they informed him emphatically was not always to be assumed in this city. So he was happy to go back and forth; between his place for a bit of vodka, then to finding a new seat, or perhaps even just standing near the bar at *Tupik* for another beer. It was a happy arrangement indeed, the location and offering, yet Alex did occasionally feel as if he was wasting whatever time he had before either having to find work or returning somehow to the States. While he didn't feel it necessary to mock up a plan, he did feel some urgency in properly enjoying his time without one.

A man on the other side of the bar gets a refill in an extra large beer mug, then begins crying. At first he hides it and acts as if something might have gotten in his eye, next tears are pouring out of his control, and the Russian words can hardly be heard over the moaning of his now involuntary sorrow. The bartender comes out from behind and hits the weeping man's shoulder: "Prop yourself up. She is nothing to you now. You have to see that."

"No, I can't. It's too much."

"It only seems like too much. You will see it differently tomorrow."

"No tomorrow—everything's the same tomorrow—there's no tomorrow, and no changes."

The bartender affectionately slaps him across the face and says, "What am I hearing? What kind of bullshit is this? Prop yourself up and stop talking such nonsense."

The weeping man is suddenly very embarrassed, and says, "Right here in your bar I'm acting like an idiot! I apologize."

"What do I care?" He pats the man's shoulders again, lowering his voice in sympathy over the

*man's shame. "I buy everyone a round of drinks
they forget it as quickly. What do I care? This is
my bar, and I look after my friends here.
Everyone gets a round on me and they forget it,
trust me."*

*The man props himself up to start drinking
again. The bartender takes his time coming
around and taking orders for a round on the
house. It amounts to about twenty orders, and
most of the people don't seem to understand or
care why they are getting free drinks, though a
few people look quickly and uncomfortably in
the direction of the man that had been weeping
after placing their orders. The man does not
dare look in any direction other than towards
the mirror beyond the bar directly in front of
him, or at the beer he is clutching for dear life.*

So he broke away from a day and an evening
worth of routine and strolled into a fancy hotel
lounge. It was time to put some real pressure
on that card he'd obtained in Glendale; perhaps
he'd feel the need to leave the hostel soon and
pull out one of his own credit cards out of
concern for legal repercussions, but for now it
felt like open terrain he had only just kicked
the sands of. Once he successfully paid for his
first round (vodka and chaser), he was not at all
concerned about the price of the drinks or what
number it was they told him was the minimum
(he could count to ten in Russian, but when he
heard the bar-tender say a number out of
context it threw him). He felt giddy for a time.
He was in what a friend of his once derisively

referred to as his "manic phase," yet he could laugh at that remark now, and did to himself, and he loved the fact that he was underdressed in the best shirt he had, and that there were people who resented his presence. He was about to buy some rich couple a drink, but they left.

He had a three-prong key to Moscow: his place for sleeping, his low-end bar, and his lounge for the occasional absurd excursion. People ignored him mostly. A day or two later he finally took his American bankcard to a machine to get a few rubles just for carrying around. Late that evening, the same bank called his room, to be sure this was legitimate. When he asked them how they found him there, since he had only been for a short time, they explained that when he called to check his balance, they were given the location of that call following their automated inquiry from sudden activity overseas. Not long after that, his cell phone company called his room and in a short conversation convinced him that it was actually cheaper to keep the phone on a non-functioning, or minimal setting than it was to break his contract, and not wanting to discuss his own irresponsible plans of abandonment of those, and a number of bills left hanging in the U.S, he thoughtlessly gave the number of his hostel, and the room as an outgoing transfer message from that same phone; but ultimately he agreed the cell phone itself should be disabled if it wasn't already.

This was how Alex came to realize exactly how much pleasure could be had by receiving a phone call from an unwanted party, and telling that party that he was in Russia. He got a call from Chamberlin, asking if he could use the cell phone in question on a wireless account Chamberlin accessed. Alex took his time reminding him that in fact Chamberlin had been forced to call Russia in order to reach him and ask about that phone: "So you couldn't possibly be too surprised that I'm here. Right? Chamberlin? Did you understand what all those numbers were about? They were about getting out of the country."

"Yo, man you don't have to get like that about it, I'm just asking about the phone, yo, ain't no need to be a dick about it."

Perhaps the one he enjoyed best was the call he received from a towing company based in Burbank. "Sir, we have your car in storage, we're going to need a payment for the past 12 days and the price of the tow, how do you want to take care of that?"

"Well, I want to take care of it in person."

"Okay, when will you be coming in?"

"I don't know—I'm in Moscow and I'm not entirely sure I'll be coming back. But I *insist* on taking care of this in person...."

Suddenly the towing truck personality showed signs of some of the same dialectal influences as Chamberlin: "But yo man, you know what I'm saying, couldn't you just—you've got to have some kind of..."

"Some kind of what?"

"So you're really in Russia?"

"Yup."

"So, is it with the military or something?"

"Nope."

"Couldn't you just work out a payment plan?"

"No no, that would never do at all. It'd have to be in person, and here I am. Do you have a branch manager anywhere nearby? Don't worry about it, I'll figure it out. You're doing a good job buddy, keep up the good work!"

9.

It is clear which direction to turn to get closer to the music one hears on Old Arbat. A metallic scent is overcome by the smell of burning cigarettes in the brisk but soft wind. Squeezing through a few bodies puts one quickly at arm's length of an elderly man with white hair, no beard, and only a right arm dexterously handling his melodica. He is now crouching, then straightening up over the instrument in rhythm with his own playing. He must blow and finger at once, and would have no time to make eye contact with the crowd even if he wanted to.

The accordion style music is one moment enchanting, the next entirely dull, droning; but it often impresses upon the listener the stamina it must take for such a feeble man, holding the instrument between neck and shoulder, to play so continuously with only the use of his five fingers. Coins are dropping into the hat frequently, though mostly from the hands of people passing by on the open side of Old Arbat Street, as if the spectacle were a required toll. The crowd itself responds with what seems a combination of intellectually curious stoicism, and enthusiastic, pulsating sadism.

One morning he woke up to a loud knock. He opened his door and saw that a young man he recognized from the front desk was there; behind him were two guys wearing ski masks. Alex stepped outside preferring to speak to them in the hall. Instead, they let themselves in and Alex kept the door open a crack, reentering his room behind the three visitors. He positioned himself standing still very close to his door, and reluctantly opened the conversation: "What can I do for you?"

They took chairs, and only the one without a mask replied, "I'm Nicolai, Nick if you prefer."

"Nicolai is fine, what can I do for you?"

"Well the walls have ears, my friend. Your performance last night, the stories you told in the lobby here, they do get around."

"I'm sorry, I'm drawing a blank."

They laughed. The two with masks took them off. One said, "We're only joking, but surely, you too, you do remember."

"No."

Nicolai laughed even louder. "Your exit, it was truly classic. We appreciate your stories very much."

"I would really like to know what they were."

"Well, it's good, you told us of the prostitute, the one you fancied at the hotel."

"Oh."

"She gave you line, you know it's a line, but you bite anyway—classic. She tell you, what was it, that she could see that there were no men around that night with money, so she didn't mind, and her manager, he wouldn't mind even if she just spent some time with you while she waited for a crowd."

She sat down at his table and said, "I've seen you here before. You hardly look from your drink but I saw you."

"Well, I can buy you a drink, just a quick chat."

"No, I had a good night, I'll buy your drink for you." She lit a cigarette and looked him over boldly. "Where else do you drink?"

"Tupik."

She laughed. "Do you know what that means in Russian? Tupik means dead end. I'm sorry that's just funny to me, to see you sitting here all the time."

Nicolai went on, "So she tells you she occasionally sees a man to the side of her business, and you told her you didn't believe her."

"It's true, I do. I try to see someone a little different, so I don't get entirely bored with men. So I can see you, only cab fare, maybe twenty rubles, as long as nobody rich shows up while we're here drinking, so I can tell my manager I

tried my best to find a <u>decent</u> paying customer," and both of them laughed because of the way she was simultaneously cutting at him and complimenting him.

Nicolai and his friends took to laughing very hard, as Nicolai offered the punch line, "And so you overheard her saying the same line to a rich customer. Classic."

There was a vacuum in his belly. He took for granted an exceptional immunity to all women following his experiences in Glendale, but somehow he felt completely gutted by the fact that a lady of the street just used the same line twice.

He went outside the bar and started kicking a tree or a telephone pole, he couldn't remember which. Chunks of wood were chipping as he laid into it heavily, always with the right leg, sometimes taking a bigger step back until it seemed he'd put a noticeable dent into it, through gradual chipping. Then he noticed a tall man in a yellow jacket standing behind him, watching. "You'll be okay," he said, and then he said something in Russian.

The man ended up walking part of the way to Alex's hostel, telling him he was local and it could be helpful in case police saw him in his state.

Nicolai said, "Yes, you remember that part, so you have forgotten telling stories in the lobby?"

"Mostly, yeah."

"Well it brings us back to the walls have ears, I heard about the credit card you used to check in. And we have two options."

"Okay."

"You can check out, and check back in by another name, or you can leave the country. One of the people who was sitting here, luckily is the first one I talk to in such matters," and he cackled with a sudden and staccato attack, "He was sitting right there with you last night when you talked about it, and he's the one who handles things like that!"

"The guy who witnessed me kicking the telephone pole?"

"No no. The other guy, the one you called the rich guy from the club. She was giving that same line to, about only needing cab fare, until you're all primed to enjoy her services, no doubt," and he cackled again. "But the man told her to say that while you could hear."

This distressed Alex considerably. "That makes no sense."

"Why not?"

"None of it made sense with her, it made no sense for her to buy me a drink, it made no sense for her to offer a date based on my having no money."

"There you are wrong. They call it a 'soft squeeze.' She just figures you can get the money somehow, and takes a chance because she tires of waiting around or thought she could take care of you quickly. But I'm telling you that's not what happened here."

Alex looked incredulously at the entourage, then mocked head movement looking behind him, "Go ahead, I'm listening."

"She did mean to meet with you, the manager was sitting there and grew jealous, and he paid her a larger cut of her share to get her to say that when they knew you were listening, to be cruel." They all three got up to leave, "We enjoy your stories," said Nicolai with a smile, "And you might want to take things a little slower with Fanya. You look puzzled, yes that's the name of the lady. I should have said. It turns out she is a favorite at the moment, and what you like to call the 'mafia,' or the crime syndicate will become part of your problem if you should happen to date her."

10.

Alex felt his brief illusion of anonymity
crushing in on him with such force as to cause
serious panic. Everyone in the hostel, and even
on the street now seemed to know his story,
and Nicolai was implying that he must stay at
this hostel or leave Russia altogether. Why
would it matter to Nicolai where he was
staying? How did Russian crime enter into the
equation? As the vodka bottles in his room
piled up around the surfaces, and eventually all
over the floor of his room, occasionally Nicolai
would invite him out into the lobby to drink
with him and several guests. Most guests were
moderately dressed, as you would expect in a
lower class hostel, though some high society
people were always there, usually standing to
the perimeters of the room. While Nicolai's
invitations were always polite, Alex had the
impression that if he refused, Nicolai would
insist, and if he continued to refuse, this was
something Alex didn't care to even guess about.

The hostel hired him shortly thereafter to
watch the front desk and do the laundry, and
the people he worked with spoke Russian
exclusively when they knew he was listening,
though most of them were English speakers as
well. The numbers of what he was supposedly
making did not add up against the monthly he
was paying there, but no one seemed concerned
about this. Alex felt certain that everything
hinged on his occasionally turning up in the

lobby to drink in plain view while relating the self-denigrating tales of his departure from the United States, and his overall disdain for American, and to a growing extent Russian society, but he also had a hard time believing this could be true, that talking loud and making people laugh was the one thing maintaining his welcome.

One night the crowd was dwindling and Alex was feeling less jovial, and more uncertain about his arrangements with the hostel. He continued to drink while the only one left at his table was Alisa—a fair, middle-aged, short-haired woman he had never seen at these gatherings before. She seemed to be hanging around intentionally to speak with Alex, who was now desperate to relate his thoughts to someone not directly associated with the hostel, as far as he could tell. She was fond of insisting that he light her cigarettes and refill her glass for her, and she seemed to take great interest in his strange predicament. She would sometimes offer some words of reassurance: "Well," she said during an opening his awkward silence mid-sentence provided, "if it were me, I would not be likely to question the reason the nightly fee and the amount I was making didn't add up. I would simply take it as a sign that my services were appreciated, and enjoy the check without asking Nicolai about it, but I do understand why you are concerned about the possible connections with the crime syndicate. It's just that usually, the crime syndicate is not

so subtle, or even concerned about the amount
of money you are probably talking about..."

But once he told the story of the hooker, the
fair Alisa lost interest immediately, and began
drinking directly from Alex's bottle. She
seemed to keep listening mostly out of
politeness, though she did occasionally enjoy
his delivery: "But my vow... my vow of low
expectations, in the presence of some flattering
gestures from a hooker; and this through other
people, who might easily have other motives for
telling them—this all rendered my barrier of
low expectations flimsy. As soon as a
mysterious possibility, no matter how far-
fetched comes crashing in, I become this wide-
eyed, stupid fucking kid waiting for Christmas."

Maybe it was how animated he became while
speaking the last, or maybe it was a funny
enough thought to her, his appearing innocent
at the prospect of a hooker's interest, but in
any case Alisa laughed, and then asked, "Do
you celebrate Christmas?"

"I don't know. Not really, why?"

"Just wondering what you might want if you're
still here in December. Maybe a night with that
hooker?"

When she finally had enough of Alex's vodka,
Alex, or both, Alisa decided it was time to leave
him with a taste of her own bitter story, if only
by implication. The accent and the liquor

worked together in a thick drawl, but her intentions of cutting into him were clear enough as she said, "So, let me tell you what I understand. You have come to live here in Russia, disillusioned by your own country. If not for your family background from here, you might have picked any place on earth. You chase a hooker, but the hooker is just out of reach. And now, without options, you get a certain thrill out of making people laugh while you drink yourself to death."

While Alex did not respond, Alisa looked at him hard, dragged her cigarette: "Welcome to Moscow. Pardon my English, if I am not saying this correctly, but I do think you'll find what you seek," and she smiled big and left very quickly.

Returning to his room, a sense of relief finally took over based on one thought—there was no way to keep him here. They could threaten him, but he could only die once. There were other cities he could visit, and as he settled down into his tomb of a bed surrounded by bottles he began to laugh, then sleep, then laugh some more; then sleep through a working shift and laugh as they knocked at his door and left. And when the phone rang he laughed harder, then pulled it together just in time to answer:

"*Ya slushayu.*"

"Alex, it's Jake."

"Jake? Holy shit, how are you?"

"I'm doing good! How's that passport coming?"

"It's very much in working order."

"I guess so!" and after they caught up on the basics of Alex's living arrangements, Jake made an inevitable case for Alex heading back to the states and checking into rehab again.

While Alex admitted this would probably be best, he suddenly caught sight of a puzzle he'd been meaning to revisit with Jake since last he saw him, in Bakersfield. "Hey Jake—remember that piece of paper you found outside the liquor store?"

"Not really."

"Sure you do. In Bakersfield, I looked at it on and off for probably an hour after you found it. It had lines on one side and words on the other."

"Oh right, yeah, something about..."

"Yeah, I finally figured out what it is. It's a guitar lesson."

"Really?"

"Yeah—the lines are sets of strings, the rows are the frets. It's blank, but it's for the teacher to draw chords. And then the back, it just spells out the notes of the strings on the guitar."

"How's that?"

"From bottom to top. The note names of the strings are E-B-G-D…"

"Yeah?"

"…then A, and E. Those are the first letters of the words on that side of the page: Even Big Goats Don't Answer Emails."

11.

A short, bald, stocky man with no beard comes to the assistance of a very attractive young brunette woman, who is carrying a heavy bag and struggling with her apartment door. Afterward, the man shows no signs of offering the slightest opportunity for flirtations. As he walks away contented, she looks at him through her door suspiciously, as if waiting for his pitch for several paces. She narrows her eyes, and finally closes herself in.

A couple weeks went by where Alex was not asked to any parties and started to sink into a routine. It was at least a work routine, he told himself, and involving some lessons in the Russian language with an older, cheerful Ukrainian lady working in laundry. There was no mention of the one shift he had completely ignored until a homely French girl named Ines was asking him to cover for her; he said he wasn't interested and she politely reminded him of the day others had to work extra to cover him, and he smiled slightly and waved her away.

He was taking an increased liking in going to the shooting range every once in a while with Nicolai. This all started one day when Nicolai was taking over a shift for Alex; one dry comment finally broke down a wall of distrust kept up by Alex since the ski mask joke took place. Nicolai was always happy to assess his perimeter for the prospect of females to leer at, and wax poetic, sometimes in the interests of gearing up for approach, but often it seemed just for the benefit of Alex and other people who were watching him flirt. Alex assumed Nicolai occasionally slept with guests (presumably guests who spoke little English or Russian, because it was not a very impressive banter Nicolai kept up in these instances) though Alex as yet had seen no morning after signs of success.

Nicolai was starting to take pleasure in testing Alex's studies in the Russian language. In Russian, Nicolai asked, "Do you see any beautiful women to fuck?" Alex understood this, mostly as a result of having heard Nicolai say it so many times and eventually asking him what it meant; but as quickly as he understood it he took an honest look around and saw an unremarkable batch of European people, mostly middle aged couples, and replied, "*Bozmozno oni v resoranye,*" meaning, "Perhaps they are in the restaurant." Hearing this, Nicolai doubled over laughing outlandishly, even inappropriately in front of guests. Nicolai repeated it several times before Alex left, saying that he was now a "real Russian," and further he couldn't wait to tell some friends of his about this joke, and when he finally calmed down from laughing he invited Alex to go shooting with him sometime.

Alex had always been repulsed by guns, but took Nicolai's offer as an opportunity to better understand the strange land he was starting to feel the need to call home. He was also growing more and more curious about what was really happening on Fanya's side of this baffling story. Having thought through his passing moments with Fanya many times, Alex still couldn't believe they were nearly as significant to Fanya as they had been to him; or at least he could not believe the version of the story Nicolai told. While Alex kept his distance from the lounge, *Hermitazhe,* his curiosity and fear compounded until he felt he would have to get closer to Fanya somehow, even if only to allow himself that harsh disappointment necessary for actual closure in his mind.

At first Alex liked only pistols. Nicolai was an encyclopedia regarding popular and rare firearms of Russian make, and having discovered Alex's preference after their first trip advised him thusly while driving to the range: "You can rent a Makarov, and there are a lot of those lying about, so it would be good to get comfortable. The only two pistols I bring to the range are my Glock 17, and the 1911 Colt."

"Wait a minute," Alex said, eyebrows furrowed in concern, "you say there are a lot of—is it Makarovs—?"

"*Da.*"

"*Lying about,* what do you mean, lying about? Have you been in gun fights where you were picking guns off of the dead bodies in your wake, or what do you mean by that exactly?"

Nicolai laughed suspiciously, said, "*Nyet,* Alex, no fights, but it's good, it's good to be prepared for one's environment. Especially now, these days, it's good. So the Colt is an old fashioned gun, I think you'll like it, the old-fashioned sort of guy that you are," and he laughed maliciously at that.

Alex started looking out his window at the cold day from which he was safe in the car's closed doors. Nicolai was not inclined to show his masculinity by pretending the weather was even remotely bearable. Having no car himself, Alex recalled taking a long ride with a friend of Nicolai's who was intent on showing stoicism with regard to the weather by keeping the heater off. At Alex's suggestion that they make use of the heater, down came all the windows to the tune of a great big vodka induced belly-laugh, along with an endless string of Russian synonyms for "Homosexual" and "Sissy" and so on. Alex was very grateful this wasn't Nicolai's current expression of machismo.

Coming home, gun-talk continued. The Makarov had an interesting story including employment during the Cold War, something about the cartridge being incompatible with foreign guns, when suddenly they were swerving out of the way of a canine, looked like maybe a wolf, and then they were hitting another one, and the rest of a pack of seven were running into the field.

Nicolai screeched to a halt, got out of the car, "*Glupaya sobaka,* better not have fucked up my bumper!"

As soon as Alex got out of the car, the wolf seemed fixed directly on him. Alex was walking around the animal trying to figure out exactly the state of the injury, but wherever he stood, the wolf's eyes seemed to follow. He could see it was a gray wolf, having hints of tan on the outside of its legs. Its right rear leg was mutilated badly by the car, and bleeding out in spurts.

By this time Nicolai was aiming his Colt at the wolf's head, and Alex said, "Wait, hold on..."

Nicolai was puzzled, "No no, it's okay, Alex. These things aren't protected—we're infested with them here, people pay to have their dens killed; we could be paid for it..."

"No, it's not...it shouldn't be...necessary."

But Nicolai was cocksure as usual, shook his head, "It would only suffer, it's best," and even as Nicolai pulled the trigger to splatter the beautiful animal's brains with a quick, final yelp, even up to that yelp the gray wolf seemed to be looking deep into Alex's thoughts and begging him to act on them.

Alex hid tears on the way back to the hostel. He was eager for a drink, but didn't want to drink from Nicolai's flask, so agreed to stop just out of town at a rugged tavern called *Strelka.* While drinking at this tavern Alex figured out that the man in the yellow jacket, who walked Alex home from *Hermitazhe,* had actually come by the hostel and left a note several days before. Nicolai was meant to pass this along, but since it wasn't a woman, more specifically since it wasn't a "fuckable" woman, he kept forgetting to mention it. There was a phone number back in the office, and with it some scribbled, complicated instructions on how to leave a message that would reach the old man.

Once Alex got in touch with him directly, the initial idea was that Nicolai would come along to meet him, firstly to "protect" Alex from any kind of Moscow hustles the old man might have in mind, and secondly so that Nicolai would have a chance to amuse himself by beating the "Sad old fuck" at chess (Alex turned down a challenge, stating that he hardly remembered how to move the pieces). As it turned out, Nicolai lost the first three games they played, and it was a very close game the younger player finally took. During this fourth game, even Alex became interested, having been only glancing at the previous games while sipping beer and watching people pass on the street up to that point; but both of their queens were off the board, and Nicolai's face was cartoonishly intense, as a result of his pent-up anger from losing before. When Nicolai won, he had barely enough class in him to contain his victory celebration to a smug glance around the room, taking note of any woman who might have noticed how the game ended. "I figured him out," he said to Alex, "it only took me this much time."

Alex saw the old man's smile and decided to try poking at Nicolai's confidence: "So you're ready for another one now—I've only just started this beer."

"Not today. He knows I've figured him out, that's enough."

When the old man came to realize that Alex thought of him in all the time before as the "Man in the yellow jacket," he latched onto the idea, though it was rare for him to wear that same item. He said that Alex must always refer to him as "Yellow Jacket."

Alex asked, "Do you have yellow jackets in Russia? The insect?"

The man paused almost too thoughtfully considering the question, and said, "Yes, we do have them here, they are very pesty and problematic for children, so it follows that you should call me by this. You see Nicolai here, for how manly he likes to pretend to be, he is really very much a child in his mind, and of course in his chess game—it seems his chess game has, how do you say, an *allergy* for the Yellow Jacket."

Yellow Jacket, or YJ, while entertainingly derisive in Nicolai's presence, spoke even worse

of him when Nicolai wasn't around. One
morning YJ was drinking coffee while Alex
nursed his hangover with beer. After a long
discussion over which beers were appropriate
the morning after drinking, YJ started in
heavily about Nicolai's character, seemingly as
a sign of concern over Alex's involvement with
him: "A man who will steal your joke... this is a
man who cannot be trusted. Very few
exceptions."

Alex sipped deeply, hoping for an answer to his
mild yet maddening headache: "How's that?"

"Well, listen, to steal a joke, one has to be both
clever, and without any moral substance.
Firstly, to steal a joke, you've got to realize that
it's going to put the other person, strategically,
in an awkward position. Take this story for
example, the one you just told. Nicolai told the
same joke as you, but you were at the butt of it.
You joked that he was asking greedily over the
prospects of acceptable women in your hotel,
or the hostel I guess, and as he tells it now, to
his friends, he was the one who said the clever
thing. It is, perhaps, equally funny either way,
but now, when he tells it, it appears to others
that you were the one drooling like a school-
boy at the idea of attractive clients in your
workplace. This maybe seems harmless, but
look again. Even as these people have seen him
act a complete ass around women, now it looks
as if he's had some hidden wit all along, that
quickly, and you on the other hand are falling
in the eyes of these easily led *donkeys* he calls

friends. All of this is to say that there is more to the little shit than meets the eye."

12.

A wide-eyed kid in blue and red overalls opens the grocery store door and smiles in angelic wonder at one's unusual accent in thanking her. She steps aside and waves with the polite sophistication of an adult, insisting that you walk past rather than take the door and hold it open yourself.

One day at the desk, Alex received a call meant to go to his room. It was a woman's voice and he spoke just enough front-desk Russian to remain disguised to the caller and take a message, a message from Ana. Ana was working in Prague on a fashion show and expressed interest in taking a train up to see him before going back to the States.

Alex was distracted at the desk for the next three hours. Feeling stuck in his routine, and still mostly uncomfortable and socially confused in Moscow, he had a number he could neither see calling nor ignoring. In the States he always felt that only one or two friends were necessary, and everyone else needed to be kept at bay. Moscow offered for him that initial feeling of absolute and welcome isolation, and then an intense and anxious loneliness, proving he had in some way taken for granted his friendships with Jake, Roy, Tatiana, and a short list of other American friends. Even if just through the occasional telephone conversation or meeting, these relationships covered his

occasional and fickle need for social
interaction, which now he had doubts he could
ever establish here.

Alex found himself reflecting on Yellow Jacket,
who had watched him nearly injure himself
kicking a telephone pole or something
repeatedly, then walked him home. He could
resolve to enjoy Yellow Jacket's company,
speaking of Russian literature and laughing at
Nicolai's expense. But old man Yellow Jacket
was someone he had to track down for at least
a day or two to hope to see; Nicolai was not at
all made of those things Alex looked for in a
friend; and he still hadn't conjured up the
courage to go and see Fanya at that same hotel
bar, if even she could be found there, or
anywhere at all.

Almost any other contact from the States, other
than Trenton or that abysmal roommate of his,
Chamberlin, would have been desperately
welcome company. Thinking back on his last
encounter with Ana, the disgusting taste in his
mouth, the burn in his gut, all the feelings he
managed to leave back in Glendale immediately
returned from her unexpected call; and yet, and
yet, he could hardly see leaving it given his
state of affairs. Beyond bored, he was bored at
the very edge of the world. This was what he
came to Moscow for—he had been accepting a
suicidal, edge of the world sensation on a daily
basis, while working temp jobs in Glendale for
months. When he started to feel a sense of
serenity through the program meant to correct

both his drinking problem, and the edge of the
world sensation so perpetuating his disease,
these all came back with a vengeance as his
long-term members of the alcoholic support
group predicted. But since he was intent on
going forward as he may, he absolutely
required the change in scenery, and much of
the time he still appreciated it. For once he felt
he had the right sights to go along with that
razor blade of sadness in his gut, but now
Glendale was back to take the scenery away
from him, such a pitiful life change as it was;
now he wouldn't even be allowed that without
Ana in the foreground; and, Alex realized,
sometimes the only way to dispel a phantom is
to gaze upon the actual person the phantom
represents, no matter how distasteful the idea
may seem. Considering all this, he figured he
either had to ignore a call that beckoned the
most morbid and burning of curiosities, or face
the woman who represented his failed attempt
at sobriety, and Glendale itself, despite the fact
that she still lived somewhere near Venice
Beach he guessed.

With no part of the conversation mapped out,
he was playing the same passive role he always
did with her: "Ana it's Alex," he said dryly.

There was a long pause, after which she said,
"So are you famous, or dead?"

"Neither one, as far as I know."

She chuckled, and suddenly Alex felt as if for the first time, he might actually have the social upper hand against her. He was so far beyond having anything to lose, and didn't care what happened. He was fearless again at last, though on the other side of innocent, to be sure.

"Well," he said finally, "I heard you were around, thought I'd call. What do you have in mind?"

"I don't know, haven't been there in ages, thought I might just spend a day or two, since we got done here and there's nothing lined up in the States right this second. You umm, you learning any Russian? Ready to show me around?"

"Umm, let's see..." he fought pretty hard to get this out: "*Yam o gu, no... tui ga to veesh?*"

"What does that mean?" she said tauntingly.

"It means, *I can, but are you ready?*"

"Mmm. Sexy."

"*Kchyortu.*"

"Doesn't that mean *go to hell?*"

"In this case it's more an expression of modesty, like saying *shut up*, or *stop it*. But yeah, literally, that is what it means."

Ana laughed and got the address of the hostel from him, then let him wait while she sorted her trip out on the same phone she was talking to him with. "Alex, you still there?" She told him when to look for her and even said she was excited to see him again.

13.

The initial magic from being in a new country for the first time may wear off after three or four weeks, but the American pedestrian's spectacle of Moscow remains hypnotizing and daunting well beyond the point of familiarity. To walk around an elementary school, for example, one might see the intertwined plastic tubing of a jungle gym feeling no sense of recognition for several seconds, or even minutes, then start to put together an interpretation in pieces at a time, as the eyes dart back and forth between buildings, bungalows, and then the sounding out of one word on the right side of the plainly printed sign: "Shkola."

The vast majority of the buildings (not just the clichéd domes with pointy tops as with the great cathedrals) call to mind as much art and suffering as function. Even in the less crowded areas of Moscow, such as the "Artist's Village" of the Leningradsky Project, the signs and the writing on the walls are always looking down to leave a distinct and coded impact.

On the train Ana had plenty of time to think, and she found herself reevaluating everything going on back in the States. Trenton was sweet, great in bed, but when all was said and done dumb as a post, self-absorbed. Everything she wanted to get away from in Shawn a few years back but worse. Drinking again, he would sit around on her living room floor with a bottle of wine and draw sketches for this graphic novel project that had been in the works for longer than she wanted to recall or contemplate, and whenever she got a little chilly with him, whether it was because of said questionable intellect, or because he himself had been slightly insensitive to her latest issues getting models ready to show her work on the runway, he would sulk rather transparently, but then act as if she didn't play into it one bit, and that really got under her skin. Ana figured that when you spend enough time with someone, playing it a little cool on the guilt trips is polite for a while, but acting as if there is nothing the other person can do to get to you was downright infantile; and damned if she was going to raise a teenager for a boyfriend; she already decided once and for all she wasn't having kids, and it was time for her to have some fun.

And then there was Alex, through whom she "met" Trenton. Ana's own sexual violence, she still didn't understand. What would have to be something of an elephant in the room between Alex and her, when she saw him, her unconscionable acting out against him was on her mind, but she couldn't see bringing it up. If Alex wanted to talk she would be all ears and shoulder for him, but when you let someone down that completely, the respectful thing is not to come trampling in with apologies and presumptions. Maybe he just thought it was funny by then, probably he was on the brink of marriage and bringing someone home.

Something Trenton said after the Thanksgiving alcoholics meeting was odd, she wondered if maybe there was bad blood between them, but knew Alex well enough to believe that if he had serious residual feelings, it would have come out during this last brief conversation on the phone. He wasn't what she would call "transparent"—he was more just heroically honest, like you didn't see anymore, in anyone. She did wish dearly she could have loved him sometimes, but alas, the unrequited loves were already his to bear, long before she got her hands on him.

The trip would be fun, she decided, the trip would be big fun. Getting ready for the show was an insane amount of work, but she stayed on top of her game the whole time. The show itself was a blast, but afterwards she felt the need to behave herself a bit, at least until she got in a little deeper with that particular European circuit, she figured. All in all, she was ready to have fun. More than that, she was ready for a change, like she hadn't felt in a long time; maybe not since she was playing the field and stumbled across Alex that strange night out with those twits from her design class. For all she knew Alex's Russian or Ukrainian fiancé had some hunky brother she could play around with for a spell; or even just prancing around Moscow with Alex, whatever happened—it was going to be big fun, she was sure of it.

14.

To fluent readers, the Cyrillic alphabet is said to differ from the Latin-Roman alphabets in how they are each decoded. While the native Spanish speaker, for example, may look at words and recognize their shapes at a glance, those who read in Russian are reading in blocks, particularly the non-cursive writing most often used for signs and billboards in the cities. Walking around and looking up at all the messages, some lit, some painted, some faded and others inescapably gosh in color and brightness—it can feel as if one is surrounded, especially in one's first few days off the plane.

Though the same sky is above those words as it is above New York, Los Angeles, or Paris, the colors within the atmosphere of Moscow mingle and taint the eyes. The toxic fumes and endlessly bright lights cities have in common seem to differ from one to the next, yet infinitely more so in Moscow, as the sky reflects back on the messages the signs sent up to that open space at an incomprehensibly fast rate; only to be sent back down making even less sense at the leisure of the atmosphere. The clouds, neither entirely natural nor manmade are therefor illusions of unfamiliar shades of purple, red, pink and black, depending on the mood of the city. One's own moods and emotions are tiny yet intertwined with the scenery; one's own thoughts, dictated by the atmosphere and emotions in response, seem more insignificant

*the longer one gazes; yet those thoughts are the
only tool available in the seductive struggle to
comprehend where one stands, and what one is
doing there.*

*All the while the smells, the industry, the
pastries, the meats; the sewage, the cars, the
perfumes and the sweat; the taste in one's
mouth mingles with every molecule the nostrils
endure and produces something at the back of
the throat—a mixture of manic wonder and
desperation as such has been tasted maybe
twice in one's life, yet it is so familiar, so familiar
to the tongue it has to indicate something
regarding one's destiny—a great change or even
death—it has to be just around the corner. But
maybe not this corner; maybe the next.*

He didn't take her to his hostel, or even to
Tupik. He heard she was flush and buying and
took her straight to the hotel lounge,
Hermitazhe, as he'd finally come to have the
nerve, maybe partly as a result of Ana's arrival.
It was quite a bit busier that late afternoon than
he remembered it being during the odd hours
he spent there weeks before.

At first he was more distracted by Ana's
appearance than anything else. The slight acne
she usually hid with makeup stood out at him
despite her expertise; her slightly crooked nose
was absolutely cartoonish; and the eyes he once
considered absorbing looked also sometimes
crooked, and as dark as ever; but he was
exceedingly aware of their darkness and the

fact that it was often he couldn't even see her pupils.

She talked about the show of course, inclusive of more professional activity in three weeks than Alex had been involved in for years. As he started to feel more comfortable, her appearance sometimes seemed closer to what he remembered, but other times began to distract him all over again. He cracked jokes, as much at her expense as his; only harmless jokes, such as what ground did she have to stand on for reproaching him a double vodka; and what on earth was slowing her down all of a sudden considering what he remembered of the nights out with her?

As he loosened up, so did he begin to relate some of the paranoia, or perhaps legitimate concern regarding what he tried to talk to someone else about in the hostel a while back— his living situation, and what he took as an implication by Nicolai that he was being held hostage, and that at some point he might be asked to run errands for the mafia.

"Wait a minute, what?" she said, and Alex regretted it immediately, but related to her the day Nicolai came in with friends wearing ski masks.

Ana remained even, but added a little punch to match the shocking image of guys with ski masks: "What? Alex, that is... you are in deep. What have you done so far for them?"

"Nothing, nothing, just telling jokes at little parties and things, but I just have this... well, first of all, the masks were just a joke, you know I think..." Alex stopped, thought about the terrorist Ana used to speak so wistfully of back when they were dating. Was this impressing her, the sick bitch, was this the kind of thing that could actually get her attention? When they were living together Alex was going to a boxing gym, and when Ana discovered this, she seemed to be acting surprised and impressed. She would sometimes even vaguely hint at the idea that seeing him box that terrorist fucking boyfriend of hers might interest her; but never so he could call her out on it, just to get him a little more pissed off and taking it out on heavy bags and sparring partners at the gym now and then. Now look how out of shape he was, and yet that little hint of dangerous involvement, just the first mention of it, had her eyes twinkling. He wanted to throw up, but instead turned to see who was hovering over him.

They were suddenly interrupted by Fanya, and a couple of her friends named Klara and Marynia. She introduced her friends as if to a huge table of people, although it was only Alex and Ana sitting there. This impersonal gesture directed at Ana was clearly Fanya's territorial statement over Alex, to which both Ana and Alex were delighted. Fanya then excused herself, assuring Alex with a seductive kiss on his ear that her and her friends would be back soon to drink the night away with him, what could stop them?

There was too much going on for Ana to remain focused. Yes she knew that was a prostitute, but she also knew the difference between bait and real attraction. Also, was it time for her to bail this poor boy out of something he'd gotten into too deeply after all these years? She'd always had it in her head the time might come, so she started thinking about living arrangements back in Los Angeles. It would mean kicking Trenton out, but she was already there; she had been there about two weeks ago as it was.

Very quickly, by way of a muffled conversation in an increasingly loud room, she learned what Nicolai told Alex about Fanya, and she started to show billowing signs of excitement at the idea of a union between the two of them.

"You like her, don't you?"

He smiled as dryly as he could, considering the feeling rushing through him over Fanya's presence in the room, "Of course."

"But you have yet to…"

"One night we talked about it, just, you know something came up with her manager, or that's what Nicolai seemed to imply…" then he paused, got a little irritable and finished, "It's what we were just talking about."

"Is Nicolai her manager?"

"No, no someone else, I was just naïve. I thought it was another John she was talking to."

"Right," she said, thinking hard. "You know, Alex..."

But then Fanya was back to the table, with both her friends, and an old rich man named Eduard who seemed to have designs on Klara. The conversation was scattered by the table's reckless use of various languages and no one being all that interested in detail, though through it all Ana managed to slip in a quick word to Alex in a manner that was familiar to him. She was daring him into something he already wanted, as a means of assuring she'd also get her kicks that evening: "You know, Alex, if money has anything at all to do with why you and Fanya haven't gotten together, that's not an issue tonight. You do realize that, don't you?"

15.

As Klara waltzed off with Eduard, and Marynia was engaged in negotiations with a married couple, Alex went off to the restroom and Ana took an opportunity to speak with Fanya frankly: "So I'm kind of looking to buy my friend Alex an apology gift. Can I pay you now, I've got Euros?"

"Yes," she said, looking away from Ana. "Yes, it's fine."

Ana was probing in a way that rendered the questions themselves obsolete. She realized it was now a dance between them, and Ana was the only one of the three of them with nothing to lose: "So you've talked to him before. He didn't have the money? You were busy?"

Fanya ignored this, named a price Ana would forget instantly. Ana kept looking to get a better read on Fanya, took Fanya's cell phone number down and this is when Fanya spoke to Ana pointedly: "So, you're going somewhere else, or you'll stay in the room?"

"I do want to be in the room, but I won't get involved. I'll keep my clothes on, might touch or lean in for a kiss or something, but I won't get involved."

Fanya gave Ana a piercing look and said, "I don't understand, you like him or you don't?"

"He's a friend, but I've always wanted to see him cut loose a little more than he does usually, you know what I mean, and it just seems like you might be the girl to get him to do it."

"So—you came here from the States. But you're not here to bring him back, you're just visiting."

Ana tried not to laugh, but chuckled a little at the whole situation. "Not at all, not at all. He's got it pretty bad for you I think. He was talking about you earlier. When he gets into a woman it's great, I've seen him like this, you'll have a blast. He's a lot of fun, I won't get in your way."

When the three of them were discussing where to go next, Ana was the one to suggest they not go anywhere, but get right to it. "I've seen this boy put down a lot of vodka tonight, I'd hate for him to do himself in," and she put a hand on Fanya's leg, and then leaned past her to punch Alex lightly in the jaw, having aimed for his bicep. Ana was also pretty drunk.

There was vacancy at the *Hermitazhe,* and all three of them were giggling with excitement as they checked in by Ana's credit card, and stumbled into an exquisite suite. There was white everywhere, but suddenly Alex was overcome with aggression, and while Ana was cheerfully watching him express a fairly innocent passion for Fanya, the night suddenly took on a diabolical essence. Alex found himself releasing the anger he had been repressing since last he saw Ana, and soon he was out of control. While Fanya was well trained for any number of twisted sexual expressions, Alex surprised her; and perhaps she was a little disillusioned from what she was thinking when she first became interested in him. Alex kissed her so hard at one point that she began to bleed lightly out of the mouth; and then Fanya made sounds of surprise that were half real and half practiced response, as he turned her with his left hand while keeping a light grip on her hair with the other, in order to change the leverage of his position. Ana drank wine and sat on the couch opposite, noting that at times it looked as if Alex was staring right at her with a lethal expression, worthy of a cheap thrill.

As Ana got her fill of wine, and grew contemplative the way she tended to at that time of the evening, she soon realized there was only one place to sleep, namely the bed, and those love birds were starting to spread out in such a way that it might be a mood breaker to join them before long. Rather than try to steal covers for a night on the couch, she cuddled herself up to Fanya because she was smaller than Alex. Everyone shifted around, unconsciously for the most part, so that soon all three lost awareness of their intimate sleeping arrangements and slept until daybreak woke the two ladies.

But morning was Ana's most sexual time of the day, and bumping into Fanya and thinking back on Alex's aggression got to her, something clicked and the next thing the three of them knew they were entangled in an odd kind of relation. It was not a three way, of which Fanya had certainly worked her share; Ana and Fanya were alternating with Alex's services, occasionally kissing each other lightly, expressively during transitions. Ana seemed almost bashful, girlish—a first in Alex's experience of her.

Alex became distracted by some advice Roy, the alpha ladies' man of all time, gave him years ago: "Have you ever fucked two at once—two women at one time?"

"No," Alex smirked, almost flattered Roy thought it was possible.

"Well if you do, don't go in there like a cowboy, thinking you'll take all the work on yourself. You gotta let them take care of each other a little, unless you're like me and fucking them both is just like any Friday night. Or Monday night. You let them get all worked up and bothered, you know, lick a little, dip in a little here and there, let them come a couple times but be patient and pick your moment before you go all out or they'll eat you alive. Unless you're like me.

Alex still thought he was seeing flashes of hell-fire in between the scenery of more flesh and debauchery than he could keep track of. He was between them, licking, then on top of Fanya, came, but when he noticed after Ana came a second time they were holding hands, his aggression came back and quickly again he was prepared to enter Fanya. Ana took from him by way of finger and tongue during this longer round; all the while she was watching the action next to her in a manner so familiar to Alex— like a brief, mesmerizing glance into her spider-web of infinite fetishes.

He felt exhausted and damned when they were through. He was beginning to develop real feelings for Fanya, confused as he was. Looking at Ana, he could think of nothing the two of them could ever want to say to one another again. He thought with any other ex-girlfriend there he would probably start having far-fetched fantasies about the three of them living together, but not with Ana, not with her. It was even stranger when Ana left to catch her train. She was uncharacteristically apologetic, looking right at Alex while she spoke: "Yeah, girls are just good for kissing, but I had a good time," and she and Fanya pecked cheeks; then Ana was back to her confident self again as she gave Alex a wink and marched off.

He couldn't bring himself to ask Fanya to coffee and she couldn't come up with anything to say other than what she usually said at this point, that she had to go. Alex tilted his head and said, "You have to? Why?"

She shook her head impatiently, "Because my manager. My manager will be waiting to see what I brought."

Alex, feeling absolutely hopeless for her, lamely touched her hair. Fanya seemed touched, but verbally excused herself again.

On her way out she said, "If you want better work, you can come to the hotel again. My manager will give you something, something easy, I'll tell him to get you something easy to move on foot, or perhaps some driving. Come to the hotel later, we'll have a drink," and this time she winked at him and he felt something in his stomach that told him he would soon be in love if he wasn't already.

16.

An old man feeding pigeons suddenly becomes a spectacle when one bird tries to pick at the food in his hand. He shakes his umbrella; the birds scatter and then return. He shakes a second time, then a third and smacks the soda bottle container (cut off at the top) with his bird feed right to the ground. Now he is an aggressive enemy to the birds he was recently feeding, as they dramatically dodge his attacks, making off with a copious meal all the while, so that by the time the man finally gives up and mutters swear words as he leaves, the birds have all but finished with what fell to the ground.

Alex had been vaguely dating Fanya every day for about two weeks. Presently he found himself lying pathetically on his stomach in a vacant side street while old man Yellow Jacket sat comfortably on the curb in front of him. Yellow Jacket seemed strangely aloof to Alex's sad predicament. While earlier that evening Alex was on top of the world and referring to Fanya ironically as his "wife to be," it was suddenly crushing him that she was hustling the streets, and that he felt he might never be able to offer her any protections from those same streets, as he was once again completely broke, between jobs, and it would take a large sum of money to take her somewhere else, as he hoped he someday might.

Fanya's manager, Anton, a short, but solid looking dark haired man in his 30s, kept telling Alex he wanted to get him out of muling because it was a waste of Alex's sensitive ear for music. Whether anything Anton said was true Alex could never be sure, but Anton based this assessment on the first show where Alex ran sound, at a club very shamelessly named, Klub Trafika. Here, Alex had filled in for Anton's cousin Evan who usually ran the board; but after that week Evan was in a detox center, Alex was left to choose between unemployment and what seemed to be an increasingly dangerous job, moving high quantities of <u>krokodil</u> or some other brand of cheap high short distances and drinking heavily with people who were beginning to seem restless and suspicious of Anton. Anton's prices were up, and as people in any business will turn suspicion against those in power through gossip, the rumblings among the hirelings were beginning to present themselves in the form of criticism of the kingpin's product.

"When doubt in product is suggested against a drug dealer," one of Anton's more articulate distributors explained to Alex, "you can expect that a general unrest will grow quickly and violently. I myself am by no means immune to people under me turning, but someone like you, someone he has been deliberately keeping out of harm's way for no real reason, you should by all means keep your profile as low as possible at a time like this."

Alex answered in an exasperated panic, with his eyebrows furrowed and his voice in its upper midrange: "Of course I want a low profile. Wait, who the fuck would care about me? I'm nobody, I just move boxes."

"Don't get me wrong," the tall, bald, and heavy set, menacing dealer smiled, spitting a cigar end so far away from Alex's direction it almost seemed a sarcastic overstatement of good manners, "You are very well liked, to be sure. But this position you hold, it is unheard of, or didn't you know? Mules are dealers. Every other mule deals, yet you are kept free from contact with the addict. No, it's not a good time to look like Anton's pet, you'd best be careful."

As Alex was repeating himself, in relating his growing distaste for Fanya's profession, and his feeling of helplessness around the same, finally YJ broke in boisterously:

"You have to understand—you have to understand perspectives."

Alex pushed himself up so his chin was resting sideways against his folded arms, and asked, "Do you think I lack an understanding of… Fanya's perspective?"

"There is nothing to understand about Fanya, because you so obviously love her. There is never anything to understand about that, for a man, Alex. Never are we better off for *understanding* the perspective of the woman we love, or the woman we desire, you must only support that perspective wherever it may turn. If you chase the idea of understanding her logically, that will only throw you off further. If you love, you love. That is all I can tell you right now, I'm..." he looked away, distracted somehow.

Alex finally pushed up to his knees, crawled to the curb and said, "Do you think much of your dreams?"

"I do," YJ said, suddenly much more interested in the conversation. "So you had one lately, a remarkable one?"

"Yeah, it was strange. I took someone home, a woman, because Fanya broke up with me."

YJ nodded quickly, dismissively, "Yes yes, you took a girl home, and you were having your way with her—and you were trying to enjoy it but you couldn't—and you were wondering if it had something to do with original sin."

Alex was surprised and asked, "Did I already tell you about that?"

"No, you wouldn't have had to," he said cryptically.

"What do you mean?" and here Alex waited patiently through some mumblings about Kierkegaard, and then some very obscure Russian philosophers he wouldn't even want to try to place the names of without a cross referencing chain of libraries at his disposal. It used to be that Alex wondered if it was only by accident YJ ever made any sense to him at all; or if perhaps YJ felt the need to throw him off the trail occasionally for amusement, but he was now informed enough about YJ's conversation habits to anticipate a quick turn back to the topic, by way of a startlingly resonant point. Along with this often came a return to firm eye contact with Alex, which added impact to the message, as it would here: "You can't expect an infidelity on your part to carry such little weight simply because you are with a prostitute. Her lovers, these are not infidelities, because of the terms of your affair. You see, your initial terms are the long standing, probably permanent terms you will hold each other to in calling 'foul.'"

YJ let that sink in for a long beat, then went on: "And you said yourself you've an understanding that those men don't threaten you. You bumped into her with a John on the street, and as I recall you said it felt as if the joke was on him. Because of your devious understanding with Fanya, at the expense of her John." YJ did not break eye contact but seemed to look right through Alex for a few seconds, then spoke pointedly, "But you have had maybe, I am thinking twelve girls for some reason, in your short life—you even remember each of them distinctly—no, you can't expect an infidelity on your part to go underestimated by

Fanya, or by you. Such would absolutely impact the relationship, and probably end it."

Alex pulled himself together enough to say that it made sense, what he was saying, but he wasn't in any shape to be giving such ideas any real thought, and at this YJ laughed cheerfully, "Well you're very kind, but it goes to show you, we Russians, we may be crazy, but we're not stupid. I suggest we eat, Alex. You could use a bite to eat, you don't look so good. I mean no offense, but you are reminding me of a particularly run-down and unhappy pile of dog shit I saw at the park the other day. This is not a good sight for me, let's go eat."

Over a steak dinner at YJ's treat, YJ felt at liberty to probe a little: "Have you ever squatted before?"

"You mean to take a shit?"

"No," YJ chuckled. "I mean for a place to live—squatted in a place that was available, but you were paying no money."

"No."

YJ showed amusement and surprise, "Really, never?"

"Never. It's not a common practice in the States. We leave people on the street, and if anyone is sleeping somewhere for free, we condemn it, tear it down. Really pisses rich people off when anyone just sleeps somewhere, other than under a bridge, and even then."

"Well, it can't be helped here. People do it constantly. If you made more money, what would you think of people who squat?"

"I probably wouldn't think of them very often."

YJ gave Alex a knowing, and slightly disappointed glare, then said, "But if you're tired of the tourists and young people in the hostels, and unless you were planning on suddenly becoming rich, which you must admit is a long shot at best, would you consider it?"

"I don't know. What's it like? I would think it's a very unpredictable experience."

"So is renting. Buying. Here, in the States, isn't it all unpredictable?"

"Wait a minute, this is what Nicolai was talking about. He knows a place, did he talk you into...?"

"He did talk to me, but in this case I am suffering from a temporary agreement with the little turd, the little *durak.* You should know what it's like, and perhaps if you go back to working at the club you can build a nest-egg by what you save on the price of your room in the hostel. It's worth a thought, Alex. You should try squatting—it's a good way to save money."

17.

Seven clowns are struggling to keep the attention of a small crowd in a courtyard near a busy street. They begin a collaborative juggling routine and while the eye may try to comprehend the work of one of those clowns in particular, it requires strenuous concentration not to become dizzy from following pins around through figure eight and crossfire patterns so intricate as to seem random at times, and mathematically impossible at others. The clowns' faces, painted black straight across the mouth as neither happy nor sad, tell of irritation with each other or the circumstances as the pins slow as a result of their reaching spectacular heights, and this becomes the finale to the juggling routine and the beginning of a human bowling act. Though they quickly yet methodically produce right side up landings for the pins in an almost geometrically perfect formation on the ground between all of the clowns, the crowd will not be pulled away from the neighboring dance, and hardly anyone applauds the clowns' outrageously difficult feats, or laughs at the slapstick of a man being rolled across cement so as to knock over the same pins.

For only a moment, you can see all of the clowns break character once again, as they acknowledge the poor timing or placement of their act, then return to a position in which to start over. There will be acrobatics, soon to turn again into juggling and bowling, all to

approximately the same sad size of an audience,
most of whom are on their way back to their
cars, and stopping out of pity.

Alex was more and more curious about his new
roommate and what seemed an age-old friend
of the soul, Yellow Jacket. He stood 6' 6", with a
robust upper body and legs so thin you would
think he should collapse. He would squint his
eyes as a regular habit, until he got to the heart
of one of his rants, and then he would look
intently, relentlessly at Alex, or Nicolai, or
sometimes one of their guests in a manner that
was strangely unintimidating considering his
size.

His salt and pepper beard was short and
uneven, but his outfits usually countered the
vagabond stylings the same beard implied. The
long yellow jacket of his namesake served as an
example of what Alex referred to in his own
mind as the "Item of Irregularity" Yellow Jacket
kept in play almost all the time he was in
public. In a wardrobe seeming on the whole to
be a combined camouflage of fashion from
Moscow and perhaps Spain (neutral colors with
some fine cuts and creases), he sometimes wore
a top hat, sometimes a bright maroon *Ushanka*
hat. When he wore nothing so garish up top, he
might sport a pair of boots with what Alex
could only think of as a strange Russian take
on American heavy metal style, with studs and
a leather strap wrapping around only one of
these boots; a strap which served no function.

While he wouldn't expect to see more than one of those "irregular" items on Yellow Jacket at the same time, to try to have a conversation with him about his choice in clothes would only result in either a feigned or genuine grumble of bafflement and exasperation, such as "What kind of talk is that about clothing, mmm? You are more American than at first I thought, Alex." Yet the pattern to Alex was undeniable—clothes fit to get him into almost any restaurant in the country, and one item very much out of place.

As for Nicolai, Alex considered him an unlikely fair weather friend, but between Nicolai and the old man, what started as an amusingly abrasive friendship with some outstandingly tense arguments at interim was beginning to turn into a reverse of the formula—out in out dysfunctional hysteria as the rule, with a few chuckles in between. Despite these ambiguous relationships, the three of them came to the conclusion the best options for each consisted of squatting in a two story, three-bedroom house near the hostel. The plumbing worked, but when Alex asked his new roommates admitted this could easily be cut off anytime; however, they assured him, since Nicolai was still managing the nearby hostel they could always go down the street and use the facilities of an empty room.

Alex settled in and soon Fanya was visiting him there frequently, and having quite a bit of fun listening to old man Yellow Jacket and his very amusing insights. One night it was just YJ and the two of them at first, as Nicolai was on a date, so YJ addressed the couple boldly with some of his theories about the two different sexes, even as both were represented in intertwined affection before him: "Women study themselves now, and this is good. Women's Liberation courses at the universities, it's good, because men have been studying themselves at colleges, churches, and in bathhouses" and he winked at Fanya, "for thousands of years. But the distinctions in predicament, between men and women, this is not studied, and it's actually very simple. I will only ever say this once—I'm fond of you two, I like seeing the two of you together, but I'm only going to say this once: women are fire, and we men, we are the fuel." Here Fanya giggled, at first incredulously, then a little alarmed at whatever her ideas were about the seriousness YJ maintained.

He paused, not offended, but without even acknowledging Fanya's laughter with a smile: "The razor's edge for women is exactly what we know to be true, of course—the double standards, hideous violence—all of this is unfathomable to most of us men. But on the other hand, we men are meant to withstand a certain amount of pain unflinching. I say a certain amount, but that's to be determined by society on a case-by-case standard. Still, it is a certain amount—nebulous to us, definite to everyone else. Generally, if any kind of suffering less than your average expectations of

a shitty day at a shit job, coming home to a
family of ingrates—if any less pain than your
basic workingman's plight causes a man to
whinge, we are, as you might say, *pussies*, or
pansies. A man who cannot put in a lifetime
worth of work when everyone takes him for
granted, he is no man at all. But if we can take
more pain than that, or if we train ourselves to
absorb more pain than that, welcome it even,
then we are pegged by society, subconsciously,
with an even uglier word than *fag* or *wussy,*
yes? Then we are silently deemed *masochists.*
Very quickly, from that point, the assumption
is that the man is a martyr, and then, if God
forbid, he should break the archetype he has
unknowingly cast himself into, and whinge
after all; if he shows signs of anything less than
selfless heroism at the face of his expectant
community, or if he should rebel against the
typecast he has drawn upon himself out of
seething indignation, while this rebellion may
attract the attention of a certain breed of
woman at first, these women are not the
marrying type. Rest assured, it will soon then
be time to leave society altogether, or try to
recreate himself somewhere else; or else he will
hang. At the time when you reject your typecast
those are your only choices—to leave the role
completely, or to be crucified."

Alex was wrapped up in this paradigm, but
then beside himself with curiosity about the old
man he called Yellow Jacket, and his choice not
to tell his roommates or anyone Alex knew of

his real name: "What do you mean by 'Somewhere else?'"

He did seem briefly defensive, but collected himself after a pause: "Oh, my apologies, I didn't mean in terms of society altogether—it's just, nothing cosmic or like that, just another town or village, you know, such as to recreate himself with another attempt. Some balancing act between pussy and martyr is what we men seek, that's all I'm really saying. And that is by far the worst of it, and nothing compared to what most women have to put up with from us, while we slip and slide along the rivers of our own identities..." and he mumbled inaudibly, and swore in Russian, then yelped, causing both Alex and Fanya to jump, "Narcissus! Narcissus is queasy from our self-importance. What an unbearable lot of bastards we are, but our plight is underrated. Ah, what does it matter?" he trailed off again.

Just then Nicolai walked in with his new girlfriend, Ranalia, a pretty young American girl with brown dreadlocks. Alex hardly looked at her as Nicolai mumbled introductions and the two of them sat next to Yellow Jacket in front of the little card table in the one chair that was left empty across from the couch Fanya and Alex had claimed for themselves. Alex was still turning Yellow Jacket's words around in his head and trying to put it together with the fire analogy: "Wait a minute. So you're saying that for men it's a balancing act between judgment of one kind or another, and neither serves every man, but…"

YJ: "It is like this bottle of hot sauce I stole from the market…"

Fanya cackled.

"…It exists, it has density, and yet as I smash it on this ugly card table," and then he cracked the bottle on the table after two failed attempts. Alex was already covering Fanya with his body, and facing away from the action, so he got splashed on his back; but some splatters of hot sauce flew across and hit Nicolai on his forehead. Nicolai did not attempt to stop it from dripping into his eye, but then wiped with his sleeve when it did, and, being eager to show no signs of discomfort in front of Ranalia, or indeed anyone, he kept an intent facial expression, as if to be catching up intellectually with the conversation; and as tears began to drop, his sleeve came up again, Fanya and Alex were hurting themselves in their laughter, yet still listening intently as YJ carried on loudly: "I cracked this bottle as I suggest a man might crack the assumptions society has made of him at early adulthood. Have I compromised the purpose of this bottle of hot sauce?" and he took the part of the bottle left in his hand, and flung more hot sauce at Nicolai, this time intentionally, as if flicking baptismal water at him, "Or is it now perhaps better fulfilled, as the tears drip from young Nicolai's face, as desperate as he may be to show this gorgeous

woman exactly how stoic he can be? So a quiz!"
and he slammed the table with both hands,
allowing the hot sauce to fall to the floor.
"Which archetype has Nicolai embraced?"

Fanya jumped in, laughing maliciously, "The
masochist!"

"Excellent!" YJ yelled out sarcastically as he
stood up, staring into Nicolai's miserable yet
determined eyes, "So we have all learned
something tonight. I will leave you now to enjoy
what's left of the show, and to wonder how
Nicolai will service this lovely young lady," and
to her he bowed his head slightly, and said,
"without disturbing her *privates*; unless..." and
he turned back to Nicolai, moving a little closer
to his face with each word, "he finally does
break down and clean that sulky—
mazokhistikoye—russkoye—LITSO!"

Everyone was laughing hysterically, even the
uncomprehending Nicolai and Ranalia, as
Yellow Jacket grabbed his half finished bottle
of vodka, stormed off with heavy boots, and
turned in for the night.

18.

Alex and Nicolai were waiting for a cab. They had just been drinking coffee at a place near the office where Alex was dropping off a package, for which Nicolai required no explanation.

But before sitting with Nicolai, and getting into Nicolai's around the world and back again explanation of why Scientology offered a more "efficient" way of understanding and accepting the modern world than the *Tao Te Ching*, Alex had taken note of a petite blond haired Russian girl of about nineteen years heading up the same way he had just come from. She smiled at him with such an expression as to put Alex off for just a moment. Though her physical beauty carried in it nothing appealing to him in that moment of passing, he couldn't help but wonder why she was acting so aloof. He felt as if he was being refused of something he neither asked for, nor would have known existed if he hadn't accidentally looked into the young woman's eyes during that quick snapshot of her attitude of arrogance toward him; it was a snapshot beginning with a smile, and ending with a quick turn back and a smirk, and he was caught; he was caught as if looking for that turn, though he was sure he only turned his own head to navigate, not out of curiosity or even habit in passing an attractive young woman; though if asked why it mattered to him he wouldn't have been able to answer.

About a half hour later, Nicolai was waving at a taxi, coming to realize the one he sought already contained a passenger, and Alex suddenly recognized the aloof girl's purple suede jacket, slung carelessly over her shoulders. He also noticed she was walking unsteadily, in marked contrast to the poise she carried when she had been entering the building before.

Detecting a possible danger in her instability, he moved quickly toward her, and she didn't seem to recognize him as she leaned against the wall of the skyscraper, snickered at the sight of him and slid down to a sitting position with her back to the wall in a considerable slouch. He was right in front of her, trying not to seem to hover, and she began sliding again. He tried to get her to prop up. She giggled, and he said, "Are you okay?"

"*Da*," she said cheerfully.

Unconvinced, Alex said, "Is there someone I can call?"

A car pulled up just then, with five large and sturdy looking classic Russian thugs. Nicolai made his way closer to the scene, having begun to take interest in the matter of both the girl and the car, and so the men were speaking to him in Russian, asking if the girl belonged to them.

"*Nyet*," Nicolai was definite and unchallenging. He said something that Alex thought meant he had never seen her.

Meanwhile Alex continued trying to get information from her. He picked up on the name Sergio, and asked, "What is Sergio's number?" in both Russian and English. Nicolai's conversation with the guys in the car was getting a little tense. Alex thought he heard the English word "Pussy," and heard Nicolai laugh nervously, insisting in Russian that no, his friend was just trying to help.

Alex lost track of that conversation now urgently trying to get her to tell him anything that might be useful in finding her way to safety, and she slurred in her almost unintelligible accent, "Did you call Sergio?"

"No," Alex said, "I still need you to give me the number."

With a sudden burst of energy and determination, she stood up, patted Alex on the shoulder with that same smile on her face he saw the first time she passed him, stumbled only slightly on her way to the car of thugs, opened the back door and laid herself down on the closest lap to her. The back door slammed, and the car skidded off without a beat.

There was much silence between Nicolai and Alex during the cab-ride home. Sensing Alex's tension, Nicolai occasionally spoke up:

"Probably the worst they would do is to take turns with her, and drop her somewhere, and the police will get her. She gave herself to them, there was nothing you could do."

Finding no comfort in Nicolai's scenario, Alex went on to voice his own, which he knew to be far-fetched all the while: "Maybe—it's possible she already knew them. They were probably her ride in the first place, and they just thought they'd fuck around with us, you know, thinking we were just a couple of kids—they probably just thought we were trying to make off with this girl, one of their girlfriends, and they just, thought they'd fuck around with us. It's possible anyway, don't you think?"

Nicolai chortled.

Alex rolled his window down very slightly, and suddenly caught a scent he had no trouble identifying by comparison: "What the fuck is that—that smell?"

"Oh yeah. I don't know what the product is, but there is some new industry that produces something like that—like the smell of man's come. It's disgusting, sorry—on behalf of my city I apologize, it's sort of—sort of ironic after what we just saw, don't you think?" Nicolai cackled, then felt Alex's discomfort, and went back to trying to ease his mind: "It's just how it goes, man. You can't blame yourself. She was asking for it—she's just a certain type, there's no helping a bitch like that."

19.

It's barely sunrise. A woman wielding a jackhammer stops to chat with an American couple on their way back to the States who got lost from their public transit route. The woman holds the jackhammer up to one side, and speaks as if the rigorous work she was engaged in had no impact on her: "You say, you're trying to find bus for the Sheremetyevo, or the Vnukovo?"

"Vnukovo," the husband of the couple says, "but we're not in any hurry."

"Yes, I see," and she goes on for fifteen minutes about restaurants, museums and libraries where they might enjoy stopping along the way. Finally the foreman yells at her from across the street, and she doesn't even turn toward him. The American couple looks nervous for her as the foreman crosses the street. "Don't worry," she grimaces, "I know how to deal with my stupid fucking boss." She laughs as the couple walks away. She starts the motor of her jackhammer just as the foreman gets to her and starts yelling again; he finally gives up and goes back toward the portable.

The most recent complaint to be made about Nicolai as a roommate was his new girlfriend. The complaint was not yet named in front of the girlfriend, but it came from YJ and Alex most often failing to keep up a sense of humor regarding the drama of Nicolai being constantly

on the point of explosively breaking up with
said girlfriend, Ranalia, about every other day.

Meanwhile, another neighborhood development
was the discovery of a corner down the street
from the squat house of great personal
importance to Alex. On this corner Alex could
find his favorite coffee, next to a pastry shop
that served coffee, but not near the caliber of
coffee Alex found next door. So he would
routinely bag his pastries, tuck them into his
coat, sit down at the coffee shop (a fairly busy
place) and eat those pastries, which looked
similar enough to the ones the coffee shop
served for Alex to be able to enjoy the whole
experience in peace. He would have a to-go cup
ready for his last refill, and cash checks across
the street at his bank.

When Alex first started getting checks from
Anton (through a club Anton opened from
private parties only, to being public on
weekends) Alex could extract no specific
suggestions as to where to open a bank
account, although he did have instructions
regarding a few banks he must avoid. The bank
Alex chose had a branch on this same favorite
corner, inside a grocery store. Not only did the
bank inside a grocery store offer proximity to
the shops he needed to start his day, but it also
had hours of operation on Sunday for some
reason; stranger still, they were closed on
Saturday. Since he would often receive his
check on Friday, he found he could mercifully
pass on Saturday rides into the heart of the city

from Nicolai and Ranalia (who would doubtlessly bicker all the way along on any trip), and instead wait for the Sunday hours at the branch so convenient to his illegitimate house.

Alex got back from this corner about noon one Sunday, and Nicolai and Ranalia's obligatory fight leading to a loud rumble of make-up sex ecstasy had apparently already been fulfilled, since YJ and Nicolai were both fixed on YJ's computer screen, which offered a split image with a Russian soap opera on the left, and a silent but captioned Russian news broadcast on the right. Alex asked if anyone had a radio.

"Why?" Nicolai asked aggressively, even oppressively.

"I heard something at the café, a radio station they said—I want to tune it in."

Impatiently, without looking at Alex, Nicolai said, "So go to the internet in my room, you can find it just as quickly. Anyway, we don't have radios in this house. Use the internet, it's got the same shit you want to listen to anyway, and more of it."

"I don't want the internet, Nicolai, I want the radio."

YJ suddenly took interest: "He wants the radio for the experience of it. Alex, correct me if I'm wrong, but if the young man were averse to thumbing through a sweeping, categorical process to get his audio, why on earth would you think to blame him? The internet, as efficient as it can be, is also a tedious sampling of human agendas, like…"—and here he paused with a pointed glint in his eyes, knowing this argument would eventually infuriate Nicolai— "It's like a box of information, I'll give you that, a lot of information inside. You put your hand in, and maybe if you're apt, it's like having a flashlight for a glimmer of a view to see your way around; but eventually you stick your hand in, and thousands of little penises will be butting into you while you search. Finally, you pull something out, because it didn't *feel* quite like a penis, but it isn't what you wanted. On the other hand, you turn the radio on, transparency is instant—gratification or disappointment, but in this house, we don't even turn the computers off when we're not using them. Who knows what little penises are hopping out of the box at night, springing from the bounce of their testicles' intentions, right into your ear for a good, juicy little secretion of internet *jizz.* Yes, very much in *your* ear, Nicolai, because you are so perfectly fertile in your *gullibility;* so very ripe with ignorance, and eagerness to believe in *trends."*

Alex was already in Nicolai's room when Nicolai started yelling at the old man. Alex quickly found an internet station playing Russian club music in order to drown out some of the argument. Soon he fell asleep when he heard laughter had replaced the shouting and swearing, always in more English than Russian between those two, as if they were performing for Alex in demonstration of exactly how poor of a fit the two of them were for living together.

When he woke up it was to the door opening. Ranalia came in quickly to grab something, and for some reason she yelled out at Nicolai, "Alex is in here!" and Nicolai retorted as pointlessly and loudly, "I know," and so Alex and YJ had the place to themselves.

They played some cards, a game Alex was just learning and wanted to play better next time there were four or five in the house. Alex was curious again, and decided to ask about YJ's real name, but YJ deflected the topic back on Alex: "I was mixed up in some things, it's best you call me by my house name. But what about you? You now go by Alex Aronovich? Why have you dropped your American birth name?"

"That was Nicolai's suggestion. 'Ovich' doesn't even really make sense as a last name here, but Nicolai promised me it would make no difference—that no one would bother to question me if I introduced myself as Alex Aronovich, so now I do. I know, I know, I shouldn't listen to Nicolai, but I like the sound of the name is all."

YJ nodded with a smile.

20.

One morning, after a weeklong stretch of daily
muling, Alex woke up and felt urgency in his
displacement. It wasn't the first time, but he
thought suddenly that he must at last realize
he really was in Russia. Since arriving in
Moscow, he had twice taken a train to St.
Petersburg, but it was a fast train, and though
originally he left intent on seeing sights and
enjoying himself during his short trips, he
ended up preoccupied by a dispute with LOI, or
Los Angeles International, the lending bank in
the case of two of his credit cards. At some
point, the bank started charging him fees for
use on the cards at places like video rental
stores in the U.S, where the card was untouched
but being kept on file for security against
would be rentals. The problem was that they
were charging a tiny fee for these services,
between 15 and 45 cents each, and then
charging 25 dollars a month in late fees
accrued while he thought he had no balance at
all, and so didn't bother to catch them up on
his mailing address.

In any case, back in Moscow, he was anxious
over the fact that for weeks he had only seen a
small chunk of this famous city through the
eyes of Fanya's criminal boss, or to a greater
extent an amalgam of perspectives, namely his
two roommates arguing over the history and
significance of what they were seeing on a case
by case basis. So he resolved to venture out on

his own, right there in Moscow itself. Frightening though some of his recent drug transactions were, he did find his pockets were lined with an impressive amount of spending money. Savvy from watching Fanya use taxis, he negotiated a price before getting into the car—a price that would take him to the Moscow River on the west side of the city.

After he paid the quiet cabbie, he started walking vigorously to combat the cold, using the river as a frame of reference to keep him from feeling he was getting lost, though indeed he had no map or way of knowing where he was. The first cathedral he stopped for was so stunning he found himself in a daze, walking around to stare at it from different angles at least four or five times before he even thought to go back along the river that was flowing underneath, but already frozen to a large degree on top. Bright blue, green, and golden onion domes kept causing Alex to stop and contemplate the creation of these objects. He had not taken any vodka or beer starters on his way out of the squat pad, yet these sights rendered a state of dizziness and awe. He was so unaware of the scattered groups of tourists that he bumped into someone as he turned around out of indecision regarding where he should best stand to take another long look.

As he touched one of the pillars at its smooth white base he considered referring to the experience as "religious," to his friends, and quickly thought on how they might enjoy mocking him. Yet by standing there as long as he did, having had no preconceptions of what he would do with his day, it was almost a strong enough argument in his mind that this was an extraordinary, even transcendent moment in his life. He had been touched, if not by an intelligent or omnipotent spiritual power, then by the long since passed-away architects who were so bold as to imagine this kind of beauty and captivate Alex centuries later. He said he was sorry to another man after bumping into him, though he didn't even look him in the eye as they passed each other.

The luxury of indifference toward other people was no longer one he felt he could afford as he approached the Kremlin. This particular gorgeous historic building was also something he recognized as an important governmental office, and as quickly as he recognized it he began to regret having found his way there.

There were sparse soldiers lined up along the perimeter, yet upon seeing Alex, each seemed to respond with suspicion. He wondered if he had happened upon a side of the complex pedestrians were not meant to walk along, because although he was subtly creating a greater distance between the line of his path and the soldiers, as his discomfort increased, to where he was nearly walking on the ice of the river itself, he could no longer deny that the soldiers were actively gathering and communicating with one another, as well as with a central office by means of electronic devices. In a very short time, he was apprehended, blindfolded, and led into an office he thought to compare with a break room at a fast food restaurant or American grocery store.

***

His first interrogator was wearing an unimpressive uniform of white shirt and black pants. He introduced himself as Joseph. He was an adolescent boy with jet-black hair and eyes. He spoke English with a vaguely, almost generically European accent, and after only a few minutes with him, Alex concluded that the boy was definitely not Russian. He then wondered if perhaps someone sent him in as a joke, or a bit of mind play to soften Alex for a harder line of questioning once he was tired or off guard.

"I am not going to pretend that you were breaking any laws just now." Joseph paused to the point where Alex found himself wondering if the conversation would go any further than that statement without Alex's help. Finally Joseph picked it back up: "I understand you are American. Why have you not asked to make contact with the American Embassy?"

"I haven't really been given much chance to ask anything. Would that be possible? I am not— not really used to being blindfolded," he chortled, "I think that's thrown me off of my senses." He paused, it didn't seem Joseph would respond so he went on, "So then I guess I will ask—I would like to make contact with the American Embassy please."

The boy laughed insincerely, "You are in no position to ask for the help of the American Embassy now, but I do find it strange you haven't asked."

"So why am I being held?"

"One of the reasons you were waiting here for so long is that we were tracking the numerous records related to your name, in the short time since you managed to take possession of a visa. Your visa is in need of renewing, but that's not why you're here either. Did you visit an American bank in St. Petersburg in order to dispute some punitive charges against your credit card?"

"Yes. I tried to deal with the matter over the phone, and they informed me of a branch in St. Petersburg."

"Well, you were reported by someone on the train, and so we followed you from the moment you got off the train in St. Petersburg."

"I was reported for what?"

"For suspicion."

"Suspicion of what?"

The boy's smile was coy at that moment, and as such a more convincing threat, calling attention to the authority hidden somewhere behind the ridiculousness of his youth: "Why should the government be interested in what exactly is suspicious about a man's behavior on a train? Have you heard of the explosion on that same train a few years back?"

"I think so. So then I'm being suspected of terrorism?"

"Why would you say that?"

"Because it's what you mentioned."

"No, I didn't."

Alex was irritable with this roundabout: "Okay, it's what you implied."

"No, again, no. All I'm saying is that there were reports of suspicious behavior around the time of that explosion. Since then, all reports of suspicious behavior by our citizens go documented so that we can use the report should it turn into an incident."

Alex saw another weak spot in the kid's reasoning: "Okay, but that doesn't explain why you followed me. Nothing happened on my train."

"Nothing you claim to know about."

"Right. Jesus fucking Christ."

"So for our own reasons we followed you as you found your way to the bank. Your internet profile shows you are interested in Russian literature, and yet in your cab you went right past the museum made of Dostoyevsky's house. How do you explain that?"

In that moment, he experienced a short lapse, having forgotten whether or not he saw the Dostoyevsky museum. Though he realized he did eventually go, on his second trip to St. Petersburg, he didn't think it would do any good for his case to quibble with them on that point. He said, "Seriously, you are questioning me about how I—? Okay, the bank was only going to be open for another couple hours, so that's it. I just resolved to go up there for sight seeing another time with my..." he was about to make reference to Fanya, but caught himself without a plan on how to cover the near slip.

"With your what?"

"My mom. My mother has told me she would like to come visit me here now that I'm settled."

This was true, but his young interrogator looked skeptical: "I am going to take a break. If you don't see me again, you can be sure I will have informed the next interrogator in line of everything we have discussed."

As Alex met new people, questioning continued, and seemed equally innocuous. At some point they put him on the phone with his mother both to confirm that she had intentions of visiting him over the next couple of seasons sometime, and also to assure her of his well-being. Apparently the American Embassy *had* been contacted, and she was as worried as you would think she should be, though Alex wasn't sure how to view his own situation, and hearing him on the phone seemed to make her feel better fairly quickly. This new interrogator, a woman baring a slight facial resemblance to Ana, was for some odd reason trying to convince him that they would only be recording his end of the conversation. This was a puzzling thing to claim he thought, as shamelessly as they seemed to be referencing far more probing research on Alex, but if they did only record Alex's side of the conversation with his mom just then, it would have sounded like this: "Well, as far as I can tell they're just following their noses. I guess it seems strange to them that I have chosen to live here in the manner that I—no, I thought I had a job lined up with the Embassy but I didn't. Oh I see, you called the Embassy, and they had a red flag about my being apprehended. Well that's a coincidence. Yes you do, you have great intuition. No no, they have just been asking questions, that's all, I swear. Yes of course, as soon as all this is clear we can—no, no, you don't need to call him—it's not a thing for newspapers or anything, it's just, really I just think they got the wrong impression of me."

By the time it was dark out, all of his interrogators were crowded in the room with Alex at once. With their book-sized electronic devices they were firing data back and forth at each other and then scrolling furiously as if in some kind of competition to create a case against him before the others did.

They generously allowed Alex to keep a club soda in front of him from early in the interrogation, and when he finally sipped it he found it was of course flat. As he sat there, trying to pierce the very basis of his apprehension with language he was practicing in his head, Joseph came across some of the details of Alex's more recent trip to St. Petersburg, specifically his meeting at the Los Angeles International Bank. Joseph relayed the details he found to this room full of what Alex decided must have been some sort of military intelligence interns, working in the context of a practicum for a program that in the states would be referred to as Criminal Justice.

21.

Upon entering the apartment building, one feels crowded by the intimacy of the venue, as well as by what seems to be a perpetually unlikely collection of tourists from various countries. On the whole it is a small, unremarkable spectacle of furniture, bookshelves, clocks, and other objects owned by the author while he lived there. One does begin to think of what it might have been like living through those hours in his apartment; particularly those hours when the author was not writing any of his books.

The second trip Alex took to St. Petersburg was one he felt finally spelled out a tendency toward folly in his choice of battles, especially battles of civil resistance against bureaucratic exploitations. In this case, he convinced himself he might have some footing based on a parcel implying that Alex actually agreed to the slight charges against his card from the video store and online bookstore in writing. The date of the charges, against the date he arrived in Moscow made him feel sure enough he signed nothing of the sort.

Fanya's warnings that this was not a constructive use of his time had no impact on him whatsoever. He was determined to take this fight straight back to the office that casually sent him away; now, he insisted in his mind, now he had something in writing that committed the bank to its false charge, and this left them vulnerable to an attack regarding their own records. He even highlighted the portion of the parcel he found interesting: "As agreed to by your signature," and as Fanya zipped up his jacket for him and kissed him farewell, with one of her eyebrows raised and a quick shake of her head as she turned away from the station, Alex was more sure of where this parcel could be found in his bags than he was of any other item he was carrying, including his train ticket or his wallet.

Alex was also intent on visiting the Dostoyevsky museum this time around, but again he made the mistake of heading straight for his errand, and though afterward he would find that he had planned to leave enough time for the museum, he would later concede that the nature and results of his errand definitely tainted his experience of St. Petersburg, museum and all.

Previous to his anti-climactic perusing of the museum, Alex's preoccupation with the aforementioned errand that preceded it had Alex feeling all too empathetic about some of the darker moments in the author's life. He read short excerpts of Dostoyevsky's biography while thinking back on a bleak day he might better have avoided by listening to his girlfriend's advice that he remain at home.

Coming off the bus Alex hiked about a half mile before he began to see the familiar Los Angeles International Bank logo in gray on white along a

*six by two meter sign in English, with a shadow
of the same phonetic message in Russian Cyrillic
running along the bottom of the sign in a darker
gray. Apart from this gothic design, the
presentation of the bank's identity was mostly
plain. The structure itself seemed to be a
recently renovated grocery store building. The
parking lot, however, was awkwardly narrow
and shared with an electronics store, so that to
park in one of the LAIB spaces seemed itself to
carry the danger of being caught there in the
corner spot nearest one of the bank's walls, or
working a many-point turn in order to leave the
premises at the very least.*

*At the early stages of his meeting Alex thought
he might actually have this bank up against a
wall. While he was fairly clear that after travel
expenses, his intentions were by no means a
matter of practicality or finances, but rather a
matter of serious resentment against the
institution's new policy. He noted to himself that
the investment in traveling to St. Petersburg,
using the very credit card he was disputing
charges against (not yet frozen!) inflicted in him
an additional sense of urgency that he must not
back down in clearing the fees in question.*

*Argon Ivanovich was a short, white haired,
balding, well-dressed and tight-lipped manager,
and the man by whom Alex's argument would
eventually be decided. The first line of defense
against Alex's claim was an Englishman named
Cecil Brennan, who was blond, in his late
thirties, pudgy and mild-mannered. Alex felt*

bolder in the early part of the meeting because of Cecil's meek, trembling voice. When Alex presented the parcel, and asked Cecil for proof of a signature, Cecil remained quiet, tapping at his computer for sometimes three of four minutes at a time while presumably flipping through computer screens blocked to Alex's view by a visor. Cecil's eyebrows seemed always furrowed, and his eyelids were sometimes squinting, and other times so tight they seemed shut. Then Cecil would say something like, "Well, we should have that, I'm just not sure it's in my authority to view it." When Alex finally asked to speak to a manager, Cecil explained that the manager was at lunch, and so Alex shrugged and said, "Oh, I'll wait. I travelled from Moscow, and so I hope you understand I'm not going to walk away until I feel the matter is answered for and settled."

This animated Cecil considerably: "You travelled from <u>Moscow</u>, over these <u>late fees</u>?"

"Yes I did."

"But sir, surely the cost of coming here is more than you hoped to see returned against these fees!"

"Well, I am incensed about the manner in which these fees were accrued, your telephone and internet customer service reps basically told me I could write a letter of complaint, and I happened to know where the nearest office was—so here I am."

*"Sir! Do you mean to tell me that you have come
here <u>on principle</u>? You've come all this way to
make a <u>point</u>?"*

"That's about the size of it, yeah."

*"Well, I have other customers to attend to," he
shook his head and shuffled papers. "Mr.
Ivanovich said he'd be here about half past the
hour, until then if you wouldn't mind please
waiting in the lobby."*

*"Of course," Alex said, and stared at him for
several beats, enjoying his temporary sense of
an upper hand.*

*The lobby looked more like a hospital of sick and
mentally ill patients than a bank. Alex watched
as what seemed like an impossibly pathetic
collection of barely functioning lower class
citizens shuffled through the short maze leading
toward the few clerks working behind the
counter to help these poor customers deposit
checks or handle other financial transactions,
probably with desperate loans or claims against
their injuries. Alex assessed that the institution
was accustomed to dealing with people who had
absolutely no means of arguing or defending
themselves from the predatory financial tactics,
and felt all the more need to take this seemingly
petty matter of his own as far as he could
without representation.*

When Argon Ivanovich reentered the building following a pleasant lunch, he smiled at Alex passing by. But soon Alex was back in Cecil's office, demanding in an authoritative manner that Argon show him a document proving that Alex had signed his approval as Los Angeles International Bank had indicated in its letter, or another document promising a reversal of the charges on his credit card. Argon was now at Cecil's computer with Cecil pushed aside, sitting at a triangular edge between Alex and Argon, who was clicking furiously, while attempting to intimidate Alex whenever he had a moment of waiting for something to pop up on the screen. Argon had almost no Russian accent in his American branded English, but kept a sneer with such consistency that Alex might have thought it was a permanent facial tic, if he hadn't seen a passing smile on the same face only a little earlier. "We were actually late in applying this small fee through the video store... oh and the online bookstore, I see. Your account, compared to others, was strangely left behind on this policy. So it's not going to be an easy case for me to make—justifying to my supervisor this return on the late fees. And so much time, so much time has already passed..."

Alex was not impressed: "I'm looking at a parcel that says I signed on your right to charge. I wouldn't have. I would have sooner cancelled my associations with the video store and the bookstore. I've said it several times and I stick by it—prove to me I signed, or restore those fees to my card <u>entirely</u>."

Finally, after an hour of all three of them sitting there and waiting for results it seemed would not be found by Argon Ivanovich, Argon casually suggested a slight change in the seating arrangement: "Cecil, would you mind trading places with Alex, please?"

Cecil looked as if he had just been fired so that Alex could take his place, but after they switched Alex was looking directly at a photo of a document on the screen. His first and last name were clearly forged at the bottom of the document, and the language in the letter stated the new arrangement regarding both the video store and the bookstore, the amount that would be charged, the reasons for the charges ("In order to secure your membership with the following clubs, as associated with the credit card they have on file"), and a date roughly five days after Alex arrived in Russia. Suddenly it occurred to him what happened: Trenton signed this on his behalf, and sent it in, probably out of spite for his having stolen the gift card that helped Alex get his start in Moscow so many weeks ago. His stomach was ill, but this was only the beginning of Alex's bureaucratic defeat.

"Alex, as it turns out, there's more. I have some unrelated matters to discuss with you, and so it's serendipitous you came to visit us today. Regarding your late fees, we understand—many people are forgetful and sign things misunderstanding the situation—usually this happens online, but it can happen this way too,

it's not uncommon. Unless of course there was something you wanted to tell me about that signature?"

So Alex shook his head, trapped into either owning up to a police report Trenton may or may not have bothered to file regarding Alex having stolen a gift card, or giving up on any claim that the signature was a forgery.

Argon went on with a malicious air of politeness: "You have been a student at several different universities. Some of them were more expensive than others, I see, but what you may not have understood while you were signing the online forms, at, oh for example the Institute of Art and Film in Santa Monica, was that these forms included a clause, a clause regarding the overall, international control of your loans' contracts. What this amounts to is that the Department of Education, having taken notice of your recent dissociation from the United States, chose to reassign your loan to an entity with more international influence than the Department of Education itself; namely, the Los Angeles International Bank. The bottom line is that regardless of the late fees you are decidedly accountable for on that little credit card, this other sum, this considerably larger sum is now a matter of great interest to us as well. It is in fact a matter of interest to us to the tune of six digits, and counting. You see the news is not so good in this country, for people, or if you don't mind my saying so, <u>deadbeats</u> with outstanding debts. While I may or may not admire you for having

*been so bold as to pursue an education in the
arts, I would be remiss in keeping from you the
political landscape here in Russia where the
subject of debt is concerned. May I continue?
Would you like a cigarette while you look over
these documents?"*

*Argon was lighting a cigarette for himself,
having left the screen open to a page that
described the details of about six loans from
three different schools Alex attended in the past
twelve years, including language on how these
were being reassigned to LAIB. Alex did not
move a muscle while he waited for the next
blow.*

*Argon kept up just enough of his polite facade
to blow smoke away from Alex's face between
statements: "The tide seems to be turning in
Russia, in ways that you were probably already
aware. Russian politics are reaching out to the
people of Russia, rather than to say, the U.N,
who were the authors of a certain worldwide
agreement regarding debt—have you ever
heard of the ICCPR, Alex?"*

*Alex barely blinked, and kept his eyes on the
screen.*

*"It's the 'International Covenant on Civil and
Political Rights.' One of the terms states that, 'No
one shall be <u>imprisoned</u>'" and here Argon
paused to exhale, "'merely on the ground of
inability to fulfill a contractual obligation.' I'm
sure you can imagine, Alex, that a bank as big*

as Los Angeles International is following this political movement regarding Russia's stance on the 1976 bill very, very carefully indeed."

Alex got up and left without tripping or showing any of the signs of weakness Argon was amusedly looking for, however once Alex was outside the office he found himself obsessively wondering what the conversation was like between the two bankers now that these threats had been so directly and effectively delivered to Alex, who only a few minutes before was philosophically concerned with a matter of sixty or seventy dollars, he could no longer remember exactly how much.

***

He felt a sense of great relief sometime while he was waiting at the train-station bar. He let himself freeze for about a round and a half of whiskey and draft beer chasers, when it occurred to him that mostly he was making his money in cash off of the street anyway. The dangers from his debtors were actually quite petty when he thought about it, and yet he wasn't thinking entirely clearly about the dangers of his work in Moscow as well. All of this finally led him to laugh to himself. The prospect of a bill, on the brink of being obsolete, and the implications that his debtors might have the option of putting him in jail, seemed to point clearly toward the need for a shift in Alex's perspective regarding his life in Moscow; but as he chuckled, he also proceeded to get drunk enough that his time on the train included being cut off at some point by a tall, dark-haired server, at whom Alex uttered the Russian phrase, "Svin'ya ublyudok." Fanya told him this was as close as he could get to saying "Pig fucker," in Russian.

"What was that?" the man asked in English.

"Nothing," said Alex.

"That's what I thought," the man said.

He went back down to the bar an hour later, saw it was the same guy, managed to get one more round off of him, but then the server cut him off again, leaving Alex a bit dry until the train's arrival in Moscow where Fanya was waiting for him.

The car Fanya was driving was a funny looking, light green, sort of boxy little family car because of some house sit or another, and when she picked him up she was in a good mood, even though Alex was back from a trip she had advised against. "Did you stick them?" she said, with only the slightest mocking edge.

"No."

"What? All that way!"

"I know, but they had surprises for me."

"Well, you don't need banks anymore, you've got me."

"That's exactly what I was just thinking."

22.

These people in the room hadn't spoken to him in ten or fifteen minutes he figured. Some had occasionally brought up something trivial, like an email Alex sent from the hostel, describing his evening to a friend in Alabama. They would talk about him as if he wasn't there, such as by asking the question, "Would this be considered valuable in placing him at the hostel the night that we were… no no, never mind—it's no good." Then they would go on typing things into their devices, showing them to one another and nodding, or shaking their heads and he began to doubt that there was anything legally significant happening at all, despite the fact that it was inside the walls of the Kremlin where this was happening. He took a sip of his flat seltzer, then caught Joseph's gaze and again tried to stare him down. He saw nothing in Joseph's eyes—no authority, no intelligence, no soul—and began to contemplate various foolhardy attempts to escape in his grievous frustration.

Meanwhile Alex was resentfully watching a rotating group of officers sharing information and chatting with each other inanely, good-humoredly even. He started to feel an aggravation build up beyond the realm of accountability. He reassessed his environment—the room was full of three men and two women, most of whom were physically smaller than Alex. It was too easy for him to

consider the possibility of over-powering the
five people in the room to keep it off his mind
entirely. He noticed pistols in holsters showing
on two of the officers' hips; nevertheless, the
assumption in the room that he would continue
to comply by patiently sitting there and
watching this process, despite the fact that all
of it could just as easily happen without him
there resulted in a state of recklessness for
Alex, and he directed it at the most absurd
person in the room, Joseph, who appeared too
young and harmless to be on the force.

"Where did you go to school?" Alex asked him,
with sudden and deliberate volume.

"That's not your concern," Joseph replied,
hardly looking up in response.

"Yeah but the thing is, I am concerned. Where
in the hell did you learn to turn that little
fucking palm pilot into a weapon of internal
affairs on behalf of your country, and what
other qualifications do you have that I should
take seriously?"

All five officers were looking at Alex now, and a
cute redhead, slightly amused, responded,
looking over at Joseph: "Wasn't it Moscow
Military Institute?"

Alex was only getting started, "Aren't there any
physical requirements at that institute? How
young do they let you in? In the States we have
what are called the *Boy Scouts*," he was now

talking to the other officers, "is that more or less the same thing?"

"Quiet!" Joseph commanded, but in that moment the room was good humouredly becoming invested in Alex's line of inquiry.

After a long, uncomfortable beat, "Oh yes!" one of the men said. "*Yuny Razvedchik!*" and the rest were starting to laugh along.

"Quiet!" Joseph ordered again. "I can report you all for insolence! Alex, answer this—if you are so unimpressed with my background, what has your background done for you so you end up here in my custody? You have a degree—in what, Art and Design?"

Alex was fuming with contempt: "You have really got to be kidding me. I've been here for hours while you go scrolling through my personal database, and this is what you've learned. That's the name of my school. Film, I studied film in school, that's the degree, Art and Design is the name of the school. You little fucking twat, this is where your research led you, after all this time? Where's the surveillance in this room?" He looked around mockingly, "Is anyone paying the least bit of attention to your work here? Who the fuck *are* you to be holding me here?"

At that Joseph stood up. "Good!" Alex said. "Finally you are doing some real work for your country," and when Alex got out of his own chair to face him, everyone else in the room pulled out their pistols. Some had been showing and some were hidden, but now four guns were pointed at Alex, though he was somehow beyond the fear of them.

The young officer, appalled at Alex's antics also felt empowered by the presence of his armed compatriots, and he stepped forward and threw a right hook at Alex's head. Alex instinctively covered by lifting his left arm up and tucking his chin, but it was hardly necessary given the weak impact of the blow. When the fist glanced off, Alex looked around the room at the guns, and rather than retaliating to his own probable demise, he thought to casually pick up the seltzer water on the table in front of him and pour it over Joseph's head, who stood aghast as the entire room resumed laughing at him with real pleasure and enthusiasm.

"Shoot!" he begged, "You saw that, he assaulted me! Shoot, shoot!" but it was no use. Alex dropped the can on his head and sat back down in a gesture of contempt for the younger officer, and also self-defense assuming he showed less of a threat to the rest of them in doing so.

The room continued to laugh, one of them lowering his gun and doubling over while Joseph seemed nearly on the point of crying, and left the room by one of two exits. When the laughter was beginning to settle, the man who hadn't looked up at Alex since doubling over finally did, and waved in the direction of the opposite exit with his gun saying, "You can go, you can go. We're done, *spaciba.*"

Alex got up, opened the door and walked through; he closed it, still hearing that hearty Russian laughter behind him and didn't look back. He walked down a long, fluorescently lit hallway, hit a "T" and turned right. He then opened another door at the end of another long walk and found ambience in décor and lighting, such as what he thought might be the entrance to a buffet. There were voices in the distance, and smooth jazz music even a little further off. In front of him stood an MP at a podium. He was receiving a communication in an earpiece by the look on his face. He glanced at Alex and waved him through to what seemed an endless series of doors all apparently available to his choosing.

23.

The long, carpeted hallway was supplied with fountains every twenty yards. These were the main lighting source outside the many rooms. The fountains were clearly not installed, but independent and moveable, rainbow colored and gaudy. They attracted small gatherings here and there of people who wanted to smoke and drink outside those various rooms. Upper class Russian men passed Alex with knowing smiles, as if he were new to a club. He hardly spoke to anyone during his first half hour or so of explorations, and this seemed not to bother the other guests, as far as he could tell.

After Alex sampled two or three rooms with traditional Russian meat-sticks and soups, he landed upon a very strange scene indeed. This room was a large swimming pool full of about two dozen pigs, mucking their way around in what appeared to be chocolate, but according to a poster on the door, this substance was actually an aphrodisiac for swine. That all but four of the animals (who managed to find their way out of the pool, to eat from troughs and nap) were in some stage of a mating ritual or another seemed to support that claim, and since Alex had never been near enough to farm life to have an opinion about whether or not there existed a manufactured or easily siphoned aphrodisiac for pigs, he decided that perhaps this was the situation.

Already uncomfortable from the sights, the fact that he was the only man in the room made him feel even more awkward; also, he was concerned that there might be hazards for the women who were sitting in chairs, nursing drinks and smoking cigarettes as if this was some kind of performance art. He sat in the last of these chairs, rather than standing in disbelief near the door, and asked the two women in earshot of him, each looking to be in their 50s and wearing sunglasses with lightning bolt shaped frames, "What kind of pigs are these?" He felt that he should start a conversation, but he couldn't imagine any more direct questions that would lead to his understanding this culture of entertainment.

The darker haired woman answered with a British accent: "Northern Siberian pigs, I believe."

The other woman said something in Russian, and they kept speaking quietly, without acknowledging Alex during the exchange. When the British lady finally turned back to him she said, "Yes, Northern Siberian," with a pleasant smile. "We were having a hard time deciding because you can see that the liquid obscures their color patterns a little, but see there—on that one that is resting, you can see the bristle a little more clearly," and she smiled again.

The pelvic thrusting of these animals was truly a spectacle, but with the number being kept here, and no one to watch them, Alex had to ask another scientific question: "Don't they ever break out into fights?"

"No—something in the aphrodisiac apparently. I guess those resting pigs have had too much," and she broke out into a gruesome cackle, and then Alex took his leave.

It was in the next room, the banquet room where he saw three very familiar faces from the States: Jake and Roy were on one side of this large table; Ana was on the other side. Ana was the only one sitting of the three, as a toast was being proposed. He thought he heard the word *Kinokamera,* or "Movie camera," and took a spot near the middle aged bearded Russian man proposing the toast. Immediately a shot glass was presented to him, and general insistence that he begin catching up with the last several drinks seemed to outweigh his self-consciousness regarding Jake sitting across, since Jake was the one who had taken him to rehab just a few months before.

When he finally made his way across the table, he was entirely unsure as to whether his friends had even spotted him, and he came to believe they had not when they finally made their greetings. "What the fuck are you guys doing here?" Alex said as he and Jake hugged.

"Oh I'm just here with Roy. Roy, what are we doing here?" Jake asked as Alex moved over to Roy, shook his hand and bumped his right shoulder against him in a half embrace.

"The host is talking about backing some stuff of mine, we're just here to hang out pretty much." But with that Roy excused himself to shake hands and chat with a couple he recognized as they were walking in. As he left, Alex couldn't help but ask him, "Wait a minute, Roy—have you seen the pig breeding room?"

"Yes," he laughed significantly, "I absolutely have. It's hilarious, I had a hard time leaving."

Before long he got his nerve up to approach Ana, who smiled and raised her eyebrows, but didn't keep eye-contact with him for very long, as this was during a toast. Of the three people he knew at the party, only Jake seemed even remotely impressed over bumping into him at The Kremlin; this was one example of what Alex would refer to in his mind afterward as "The Glaring Inconsistencies" about this two-day party.

There seemed to be infinite rooms, and he never perceived any discouragement while entering them. Most were set up like lounges, and seemed to be mixtures of people from a certain European country, although there was one room with Japanese guests. Alex could swear the drinks were watered down as a rule; or perhaps oxygen was being fed into the rooms somehow, because he was perpetually coherent enough to introduce himself to strangers, and get laughs from one or two jokes he kept recycling, since again there were so many different mixtures of people. Over time, he didn't fall asleep, but began taking rests in these rooms, reaching something like a catnap state while listening to people from all over the globe talk about what seemed to be unimportant and apolitical matters across the board. Soon enough, Irish coffees and lattes took precedence over cocktails, and breakfasts were being offered wherever he went, though the central room was now empty, and he hadn't seen Ana strolling casually through the hall in about four or five hours.

Whenever he had a chance, he did disclose to various people at the party how he happened to arrive there, including the interrogation in an adjacent section of the same building. The most encouraging counsel on the matter came from a Chinese businessman who was in a huge five star hotel style bedroom suite full of Japanese business class guests. The beds were left untouched, but the room was otherwise very full.

Li was a tall and thin, casually dressed man in his forties who would remind Alex that he was Chinese, not Japanese several times, and with a quick smile as if to save Alex the embarrassment he was right on the point of creating for himself, though Alex was only hanging on Li's every word (interrupted frequently by his gorging on sushi from a new plate of it brought to their little nightstand sized table every ten minutes) because he seemed to understand that Alex was both uncomfortable and incredulous regarding his own legal situation.

For the moment, Li was working on shrimp: "You must not fill up on shrimp. It's tempting, but a bad idea. So much of the best stuff will come in the next round, but me, I can keep eating. That's the advantage of my size. I'm sorry, I was just about to ask you something I think may be pivotal, as to your being allowed to stay here. I understand that you have friends who are guests, but it's unlikely they would be able to protect you in the case of escaping from an interrogation, unless of course these friends are more influential than you imagine. You say that this Roy, from Los Angeles, he is a writer?"

"Yeah. Starting to see returns from Hollywood I think."

"Hm—well you know, even Russian politicians have no built in, magical immunity to Hollywood. It's possible that he may have been able to put something like this together."

"Put what together?"

"A fake interrogation. I mean presumably they were going to get in touch with you, these friends of yours, correct?" Alex squinted, Li went on, "So maybe this was a... what you call *practical joke* I believe?" Alex nodded quickly and Li paused, then looked right at Alex: "It could be possible they meant to play around a little bit, but the people they got to play these roles, maybe they got caught up in the joke, you know, carried away."

"It's hard to imagine Jake involved in such a thing, but it's possible."

"I don't know what your relationship is with them, but if you can't just flat out ask them, then, I would say maybe…"

"No no, these are dear friends. I can just come out and ask them," but the next couple times Alex saw Jake and Roy, he found he could not. There was a natural flow of conversation and humor between them that always seemed to take over when they were reunited, and Alex found that whenever he was considering asking them if they arranged for his "invitation" to the party, he simply couldn't without breaking that flow. Moreover, he couldn't quite think of how to put such a question, in that it was right on the edge of psychopathic behavior to allow him to be blindfolded by fake M.P.s in the name of a party prank. Alex figured it might very well be that Roy especially would be insulted by such a suggestion, since he was the "influential" one out of this pair of friends. To tell the story, or to try to lead up to this theory of Li's, that a joke Roy and Jake originally considered harmless went very much overboard, and even led to a phone conversation doubtlessly scaring the Christ right out of Alex's own poor mom, pushed the topic out of the realm of approachable.

And what of that conversation? If the embassy had already been involved, the joke theory fell apart completely. He resolved that he would have to corner Jake at some point. Jake himself had seen Alex obsessive and paranoid over the silliest of things, and so certainly Jake would help Alex at least in creating a categorically plausible and implausible sorting of possibilities.

Alex finally found his way to a chat with Ana, though it was only an aside for both of them. Ana was caught up in a conversation about the history of funk and soul music with an old Japanese couple, and Alex was keeping an eye out for Jake, who kept slipping away. When Jake was finally available, their conversation was also cut short, and then hours went by during which Alex could find neither Jake nor Roy.

Alex noticed a new wave of guests at the party, the most visible population in the main dining room area, a small group of what appeared to be African royalty. When Alex walked past he noticed they had only a few Russian guests at their table. Two beautiful African princesses leered at him ambiguously, and he got as much as a nod from the man at the head of the table whose very colorful garb distinguished him from the others, perhaps as a king.

Wandering around, still without much of an idea about the layout of the place, he was swept up by a sense of invulnerability in finally catching sight of Jake and Roy again. Roy had a cigarette going and Jake was laughing—they were just outside the pig room. As Alex got closer to them, he brushed past several people he thought looked familiar and one he thought had previously been in the room interrogating him. Then he saw another man so hauntingly familiar he had to stop. The man stopped as well, but it wasn't until they turned away again that Alex put together it was Argon Ivanovich, the upper level manager Alex met at Los Angeles International. He considered chasing him down for any more clues about the reason for this gathering, but instead he caught the end of a story Roy was telling. He was sorting through a bunch of junk-mail, including tiny residual checks from some television writing he had long forgotten about, mixed in with bills and other things. The punch line was he almost ended up throwing away a check for twenty thousand dollars.

"So Alex," Roy said leadingly, "how is your second day here at the Kremlin going?"

"Is it my second day here already?"

Jake excused himself.

"Where the fuck does he keep going?" Alex asked.

"I don't know. I think he's got business with *Kenya*," and they both laughed. "But really Alex, how are you doing here?"

"I'm doing all right. Something strange came up with the law; I don't..." he shook his head. "They mixed me up with somebody, or some shit, I really don't know."

"I think I heard something about that, that's what I was hearing. But here you are. You sure everything's all right?"

"I guess," Alex grimaced, thought it over and answered more definitely, "Yeah I'm fine. It's fine," and he smiled weakly and shrugged.

"Well that's good. That's real good. How about otherwise? You having a good time in this part of the world?" Roy shook his head ironically, "You... *happy*... here?"

"Yeah, well I mean it certainly is very stimulating."

Roy chuckled, looking Alex over carefully. "And sexually... how is Russia comparing to say Portland for you? Favorably?"

"Oh yeah—*favorably*—that it is."

Roy laughed again, studying Alex's face curiously until he excused himself, and began walking in the opposite direction from which Jake had started away.

Then Alex resolved to find out where Jake kept going. He didn't typically like mingling with strangers so it seemed odd that he would walk away for long periods of time.

Alex was less polite in getting by people and managed to catch up with Jake before he disappeared entirely. It turned out that one of the rooms in the party itself was deemed Jake's. This was something Roy assured him when describing the event and convincing him to come along, Jake explained. It was a room with a pool table, a refrigerator, and an air mattress. "Why the air mattress?" Alex wondered aloud. "Just a preference," Jake replied, and they both laughed easily. Before engaging in any pool playing, Alex decided he would switch from hard liquor to beer. The 'fridge contained nothing but Bud Lights in perfect rows of six, and a half of a sandwich of some kind on the bottom rack.

The conversations were in reminiscence of the car going through the house and other outrageous scenarios even further back, when Alex had been staying at Jake's place for the most part, but when Alex mentioned the interrogation, nothing Alex said seemed to surprise Jake, which was strange enough, but the questions Jake chose to ask seemed even stranger.

"Wait a minute, you were pulled off the street, or a train?"

"I was just outside here" and he pointed, "just outside the Kremlin. They were asking me about a train ride I took a couple weeks ago, as soon as they took me under investigation."

"And the credit card, you said—they somehow called up your student loan file?"

"Yeah."

"And you just left?"

"Yeah."

Jake nodded, but he was thinking harder than usual. Suddenly he stopped playing pool: "When you got taken in by the police in Glendale, and we called Trenton to go and get you, did you say something about a police officer with a whole lot of fur on his face or something?"

"Yeah."

"And did you ever come to any kind of opinion about what was happening there?"

"Well, I assumed he was somehow hired despite an anti-social refusal to shave his abnormally active hormones. I just figured he was a circus freak that landed up on the force somehow."

Jake replied heavy in thought, "Yeah I guess that would make sense."

It was Alex's turn to ask questions: "Jake, you've got to tell me what the hell you're doing

here, I mean really. It's good to see you but—
there's no casual explanation for all of this that
doesn't get me feeling really paranoid."

"Well," Jake said slyly, in a familiar manner that
was meant to kind heartedly derail Alex from
traveling down a train of thought that was
unproductive, "this..." and he looked around
with mock suspicion, "...this is not exactly the
place to be discussing such things if you catch
my drift."

They both started laughing, and didn't stop for
probably thirty seconds, but for the first time
in Alex's life, he wasn't entirely sure the two of
them were laughing for the same reasons. Jake
beat him mercilessly at a "house rules" game of
pool, where it made no difference what you
were aiming for, and they kept the conversation
casual the rest of the time. Alex lay down on
the floor and took a nap then. Jake was
finishing that sandwich last Alex saw, and when
Alex woke up it was to Jake's phone ringing.
After a quick chat Jake said, "Well, looks like
we'll be heading out. You want to say 'bye' to
Roy?"

Roy was to be found right next door it turned
out. He was putting on a vest and his boots,
and spoke to Jake: "I don't know why I brought
these boots, I spend half my fucking time at the
airport taking them on and off," and Jake
laughed as if there were a story or two behind
the comment. Alex was still giddy from the
booze and the unexpected company under the

circumstances, and Roy repeated an inside line
of a joke Alex hadn't heard in a very long time.
It used to be Roy would say this ironically,
because given how social he was in pushing his
writing to the entertainment industry, it
seemed an always more unlikely claim each
time Alex heard it, with Roy's finger pointed
straight at him and expression on the edge of
Dionysian in its irreverence: "I'll see you
directly." Alex doubled over laughing, hugged
them both and watched the exit door they took
for his own reference, all the while noticing
pangs of sadness at their departure, and panic
returning from when he had been apprehended
in the same building.

He looked around, but still seeing no sign of
any of the few people he felt some kind of
social connection with, he grabbed what he
thought might be just one more serving of
sushi from the room of Japanese hosts and
started toward that exit. He walked past Cecil
from Los Angeles International, decided not to
stop on his way back through the main dining
hall when he spotted a profile he thought he
recognized as Ana's, and indeed it was. She was
only finishing a conversation with one of the
party from Kenya, and smiled pleasantly while
he waited for a turn to speak, though the man
from Kenya took quite a bit more time to finish
his thought than Alex felt comfortable standing
around for; and he did not acknowledge Alex
before walking away from them.

"Well shit," she punched him on the arm, "it's good to see you again. I would've called but really this is my whole agenda, I'm back tomorrow to the States."

"That's all right, I've been pretty busy myself," he more or less lied by omission of his own disorientation. Had he been busy? Was that the right word?

"So how is it going—how is it with your friend? Fanya is it?"

"Yeah, we're still getting to know each other."

"That's great, that's great." She raised her eyebrows and said, "I saw the way she looked at you and I knew right away this was the real thing, and all I needed to do was get out of the way."

"Ana, I'm sorry to change the subject, but would you mind leveling with me, seriously about this party? What is the fucking deal here, really, I've been asking all night."

"Right?" she said looking around, though to Alex she was not appropriately impressed by the unlikelihood of it all.

He went out on a limb, despite that it was obviously not something Ana wanted to talk about: "Seriously—there is no good explanation for this I can think of that adds up—and my day to day in Moscow has been tenuous enough as it is." Ana smiled understandingly at this; it was as if she was stumbling over a private joke about Alex's idiosyncrasies she had to get past before listening to anything more. Alex swallowed this and got back to his question: "I've seen people from L.A, people from a bank I went to fight charges against in St. Petersburg; can you please just tell me how you became invited? Maybe that will shed some light."

"Well, without blowing myself out of proportion," and she offered a quick, modest smile, "I have been working on a new line that is a big deal in Europe, specifically. Colors, colors that are out of sync with the eye's expectations, like, orange... yellow, on an otherwise neutral outfit. Anyway, long story short networking is about all I have done other than design since we were living together—and if I never apologized for that time I really have meant to—there's always been something sacred about you to me, I can't explain it, but there has and you have caught me at some of the flakiest corners of my life and I just, I'm sorry to jump around but I just had to say that since we're here."

"You already apologized about that once, Ana."

"And you already deflected it once...Alex," and she smiled on one side of her face.

Alex was not happy to be off the subject of the party, but was glad to have a moment with Ana. He suggested they go get drinks and soon found they were leaning into each other, hovering over one of the decorative fountains all by themselves, almost flirting like old times.

"Alex."

"Ana."

"So you're tripping out about this party?"

"I was arrested in there, and now I am having drinks with you here. It's weird, I can trace the details of what happened but I'm still not entirely in…"

"Yeah," she said, again with a line on something about Alex, specifically, not so much about the situation but on him.

"*What?* Ana, out with it."

"Alex, I may not have any answers about what happened today, but I think I do have an idea what's going on with you. You have a great mind, one in a million, and I'm not just saying that. Anyone, Alex, anyone who catches sight of you can tell there's a lot more going on than there is with most, and some of us can tell that it's important, what's going on up there," and she tapped lightly, lovingly on his skull with her empty hand by getting up on tip toes. "All anyone would have to do is watch you listening to a spectacular, intimate live music performance—and by watching your face we know, we know there's too much going on for one guy."

"So how does that explain all this?" he said, looking around again at the international fiasco.

"It doesn't, but it could be a clue about *why* you're here. The problem isn't when you're alone, Alex, you can handle all of that on your own, and I see that, I get it, and it's great. The problem is when you bump into anyone else, in all your relations, you start from right there," and she tapped his skull again, just slightly more emphatically, and less lovingly, "you take that whole thing and expect us to be right there with you. And it's just not entirely fair."

"Not fair, not fair—what do you mean? Not fair to…"

"Not fair to you, Alex. Because then we can't help. We can't do a fucking thing for you, because we…" and she took a couple of steps back to get her thoughts together when they both noticed someone was listening in.

A short man with ghostly gray hair who was heavy, though not unhealthy looking touched Ana on the shoulder from behind. "Excuse me madam," and then he stepped between Ana and Alex, "I'm terribly sorry to interrupt."

"What's that?" she said, looking inquisitively past him at Alex.

The man spoke looking directly at Ana, though his words were meant for Alex: "I am going to have to have a word with you now, Alex. I can't tell you how long it will take, but I'm sure the lady will be around for the duration of this extravagant celebration, so, if you'll excuse us," and he showed Ana a badge at which her eyes widened and quickly disappeared back into the crowd.

At this the man turned, "Alex, will you follow me? *Pazhalsta,* follow me."

It seemed a much longer walk back to the interrogation room than Alex recalled it being when he left it a couple of days before. A sinking feeling, from anxiety to terror was expanding through his stomach and chest the whole way back through the elegant rooms, then in that return to the terrible lighting of the halls finally leading back to the office where he sat currently in front of a man who would reveal his name at his own leisure.

The problem was, Alex thought, he no longer felt innocent. Though he knew that he was not a terrorist, he was now a drug dealer, or trafficker anyway (a fine line as he had come to realize, having seen the results of his trafficking in that poor girl who was picked up by those thugs just outside the building of his own delivery), and he also knew that he had basically assaulted a young officer of some sort before he went strolling away, albeit at the

command of another officer. Everything he saw
and did at the party seemed so entirely immune
from the law that the very idea of coming back
under legal scrutiny was shocking enough; and
this man, this man before him possessed the
most intimidating appearance and demeanor he
had ever been required to look back at. The
officer waited, tapped at his watch, looked back
at Alex, while Alex tilted back in his chair with
the same belligerent posture he kept up during
most of his first occupation in the same room;
but it was a hollow belligerence. Alex's usual air
of self-righteousness was somehow stripped
bare by the gaze of a man who spoke with a
thick Russian accent: "I am officer
Strastakovich. You will never find the need to
call me by anything different."

During the next long pause, Alex kept his hands
clasped one in the other, to discover that he
was actually shaking from fear. He was relieved
when officer Strastakovich finally broke the
silence: "And anyway, Alex, there's no real need
for me to introduce myself. You are impressed
enough, I am sure, by the fact that you were
here, you are here, and haven't been tortured,
or shipped off for labor in Siberia. These things
happen as often as not, to terrorists, and those
suspected of terrorism."

Another pause and then Strastakovich went on:
"The truth is Alex, while the first line of
questions you faced occurred by way of a very
inefficient bunch of officers, there were some
things they stumbled on that came up after you

left, and here you are, still in the building after all. *Kakaya udacha!* What luck! The questions I have for you now cannot be answered by means of simple factual, true or false, or this kind of statements. They date back to an email you began composing, but never sent to Ana—the lady I just saw you with. The email was in your 'draft' box, maybe two weeks ago—the typing that went into that draft was then sent to your deleted files, but never released from there."

"Strange."

"What is strange?"

"The whole thing, go on."

"The language in that email left some questions in my mind, not so much about your behavior in this country so far, but more in a general way about your—well, let me restate that. We are not *concerned* about your behavior so far, even the more debauched involvements with some of the good citizens here—that woman at the hostel you worked with, who was supposedly giving you lessons in Russian."

"I was... I did have lessons in Russian with a woman at the hostel, yes."

"She spoke openly about your relations, and showed us the bite marks on her thigh. Here," he clicked at his watch, and on the wall behind him appeared a bright photograph of an otherwise very healthy woman's thigh with bite-marks in three different places. "I'm sure we can check the dental pattern, but meanwhile..." and he touched his watch again to make the image disappear before Alex could even come to terms with the accusation.

Once he did take in the implication, he figured perhaps it was his tutor's thigh, Alex had no way of knowing, but he felt a sudden wave of aggression Strastakovich was perhaps counting on as he continued to prod at Alex: "My concern is any potential threat to the Kremlin. Not just a current threat, but a potential threat, and here you are, having come to a party at the Kremlin without an invitation—and yet you seem to know several people here after all. It's funny, you can understand that I find it suspicious."

Alex was stuck on the last point: "I was never intimate with her. Is that really part of your concern? I was not. I encourage you to check my dentals against those bites...if you really believe I bit her, or had anything more to do with her than those lessons."

"We might, but this is only one of many items of psychological concern. Do you remember starting and never sending the email? Let's go back. Did you start an email to Ana, the woman from the party, a month or two ago?"

"Yes, I recall."

"What do you remember about it?"

"Not much. I think I was trying to clear the air a bit. I'm sure there was some anger in it, but mostly I thought I was looking to liberate myself of some past grievances with her."

Strastakovich had more than a hint of mockery in his tone: "And did you settle the matter in your mind, without sending the communication to her?"

Alex's voice was bone dry: "I don't see what this has to do with any suspicion of terrorism." Alex paused, thought, said, "Is Ana involved in some—is this to do with her ex-? Oh! That's it, the word 'terrorist' must have come up in my email, because of her ex-boyfriend! The man she was dating before in Los Angeles. Was that the red flag?"

Strastakovich simply shook his head at Alex's grasping suggestion; he then went on with a hideous smile: "We are going to conduct a few psychological assessments of you. As I said originally, I haven't any idea how long they will take because from the start of the evaluation, any answer can close a door of concern, or open another hundred doors. All I can tell you is that if you happen to leave this room again without my *clear permission,* you will not find your way to any party." He lit a cigar as he left Alex alone in the room.

***

In the hour that he was waiting, Alex spotted a clear bulb on the ceiling. Since it seemed to serve no purpose he came to assume it was a camera. Every once in a while he grimaced in its direction while he considered what might be in store for him.

The woman with red hair, the cute one he was developing a bit of Stockholm syndrome for came in with her hair down this time, rather than tied back as it had been.

"*Privyet*," she said. "Just a passing question or two while we wait for the materials, for the other part of test. Were you ever arrested in the United States?"

"Yes."

"In which of the States?"

"California. Glendale, California."

"Did you stay the night?"

"No."

"Who was it that picked you up from jail?"

"A guy named Trenton."

"Okay, just the questions I've been prompted to ask, that's all, there's no need to be cross. No other arrests before that?"

"None."

"Okay, I think what happens next for you is not so bad. I think some people will come to ask you, maybe Officer Strastakovich, maybe they ask you about your responses to some things on the screen. But I do have to connect you with this machine." She put a collar around him. "This is to monitor your pulse and such during the questions," and she smiled at him reassuringly. "I am going to check now, to make sure it's working properly. They will tell me from the answers you give and the read of the machine, back there," she pointed to the door where Joseph had exited after being humiliated. "What are your feelings regarding the following thoughts. The Kremlin?"

"It's not what I expected, but very impressive, inside and out."

She smiled again. "How about Trenton?"

"He's an idiot and an asshole, but I figure I've settled my peace with him. We're done, the two of us."

"How about the woman you were visiting with in there, the woman called Ana?"

"I've had my—I don't really know exactly how I feel about her. I don't know what I think of her, and so my feelings toward her are very confused. I haven't worked them out and I don't particularly care to."

"So are you in love with her?"

"No."

"But you were?"

"Probably, yes, I probably was. But I've never been able to say I knew her very well. I am completely stumped regarding what I think of her, or what she meant to me before."

When Strastakovich came back he was sipping from a seltzer of the same brand that Alex dumped on Joseph's head. He also seemed to have the results of the heart monitor, located around Alex's neck, coming directly to his watch as often as he was checking it during the interview. He flipped a slide show for Alex, usually of three images at a time, numbered one through three. Alex was meant to choose a preference between the items, for example he started with clothing samples: "Would you say you have a discerning taste in clothes?"

"No."

"How would you describe your taste in clothes?"

"I wear long sleeves when a lot of people think it's warm out."

"Look up at the wall," and there was then a blue screen, then a picture of a baseball cap with an

American flag, an Ushanka hat of tie-dye, and a light brown colored fedora Alex had no trouble choosing among the three. As the slideshow went on Alex let his guard down some, thinking the whole thing was just a scam or a waste of time again, when suddenly he switched to another slide and Strastikovich moved his chair closer to Alex and stared menacingly at him. There were three jackets, sported by three different Russian male models, and one of them Alex could have sworn was a younger looking old man Yellow Jacket, wearing that very yellow jacket Alex had named him for. The others he couldn't pay any mind to as he tried to figure out what Strastakovich's angle was.

After that slide, he saw other items in the mix that related back to his current living arrangement. Nicolai's beat up car was one of the options of three Russian cars, and then Ranalia's car was in another set. The young Yellow Jacket appeared in another slide, wearing the studded boots Alex recognized immediately from YJ's wardrobe back at the house. All Alex could think was Strastakovich had nothing but was trying to push him into breaking his front, by using images familiar enough to him to loosen Alex's nerves into an outburst, which would open him to questions about these same people he was living with. He began to flinch internally at every slide, fearing it would relate to Fanya or Anton, but he never saw or heard a reference to either of them.

He played along without mentioning any of
these people, or the squat pad, and so while
soldiers such as had captured him before led
him out of the building, he felt as pleased with
his performance as he could imagine being
under the circumstances.

24.

*The bus driver's aggressive tactics in getting
through traffic enrage the drivers of smaller
vehicles at nearly every turn. Sharp turns have
everyone adjusting their balance points on the
seats and in the aisles, which is done without
any change in facial expression, no matter how
great the necessary physical change of position.
Someone drops something—he sizes up the time
he has before the next turn, retrieves it and
returns to his seat, and no one pays any mind of
him or the object all the while. To the back,
faces are buried mostly in newspapers and
books, and remain that way regardless of what
sort of character may walk in and start talking
loudly at the front of the top bunk of this double
decker. Most of the people at the front, however,
are socializing boisterously, and without any
concern over what the comparatively solemn
crowd at the back may think of their antics.*

*A teenaged Russian girl breaks a pink barrette
while trying to adjust it, looks at the two useless
pieces and tosses them out the window quickly
and thoughtlessly.*

When he got back to the house, Alex blurted
out the fact that he had just spent the last 48
hours or more at The Kremlin, hardly yet
believing it himself. Only Yellow Jacket looked
up. Nicolai, using that irritatingly and infinitely
unimpressed tone kept his eye on his book and
said, "Oh really? You were at that party?"

And there it was—another moment Alex felt
that all he should have to do would be to poke
himself to burst the bubble, and the illusion of
life would bust with it; he might then find
himself dreaming, or perhaps back in rehab,
hallucinating after all. There was no way he was
going to accept that parties like that were
thrown at The Kremlin as a matter of common
practice.

Yellow Jacket said, "You should have called us.
If we knew you were there we might have come
by."

It had been a very long time since Alex slept, to
where he no longer even felt drunk, but his legs
were aching and his feet felt prickly, and he
could see that like the interrogators from
before the party, his roommates were not
nearly as interested in an explanation for the
past few day's events as he was. He was
suddenly very attracted by the idea of lying
down, and thinking on this later, or much later,
or never, but sleeping was all he could think of,
as he headed to his room.

He lay down, and for a minute or two enjoyed
that warm flow of dreams just around the
corner; where he was still awake but whatever
he was about to dream of was making sense; in
this case it was a series of quick realities
different from his current life yet somehow
very plausible—he saw himself winning on a
game-show consisting of questions about the

Los Angeles punk scene of the 1970s; then suddenly he was swimming in the Moscow river in a lovely season he never imagined finding in Russia, where even the water was warm; but then a thought hit him like a splash of ice water—Nicolai and Yellow Jacket had to have been bluffing. Even though they identified the event as having something to do with a party, it had to be a bluff. Indeed Nicolai could never be impressed by anything. You could tell him that it was currently raining thousands of pigs and all other kinds of livestock, cross-fornicating from God's blue skies all over Europe and Asia, and he would say he saw it coming all along, with eyebrows furrowed and a quick nod of the head implying that he was insulted you might think otherwise, and irritated you would waste his time with something so obvious while he was trying to play a violent video game. But of course when Alex came home, he was reeking of booze, and had been out for quite a while, so in that instant Nicolai and Yellow Jacket must have come to a silent mutual agreement not to show any sign of surprise upon hearing of Alex's whereabouts or events for the time he was out of the house. Alex was fairly certain of this conclusion in his delirium, but not quite certain enough that he could go without testing it.

He came out of his room quickly and walked over to Nicolai almost aggressively: "How did you hear of the party?"

"*Shto?*"

"At the Kremlin, who told you?"

"I don't care, I don't remember—it's not uncommon."

"But I was—I was arrested."

"So?"

"So that's how I got to the party. I wasn't invited; I was apprehended. I would like to know what the fuck—" but his outrage was weak again from exhaustion, and his sincerity suffered to the onlookers that were his roommates.

Nicolai shrugged, as if he had absolutely no idea how to help Alex, and went right back to his book.

Alex, furious again, turned to Yellow Jacket, who got up and grabbed his maroon *Ushanka* hat and dress coat, which were both hanging on a stool by the door. "Well, Alex, it is clear you need some sleep. It's what we all need after a, how you say from New York English, they like to say, a *ringer.* You have had a ringer with the law. It's time for bed, my friend. Nicolai, you better give your new girlfriend, what is her name, anyway, you better buy her some flowers, I think, or she'll be back on the market."

Nicolai got up suddenly. "Really? Oh, all right, I see what you mean. But flowers? What the fuck do I know about flowers? You'll help me pick them out."

And that was it—Alex was again sure that both his roommates were completely full of shit bluffing about any previous knowledge of the party, until Yellow Jacket opened the door, letting Nicolai out ahead of him, then muttering out of the side of his mouth, "So how did you like the *pig fucking* room?" and he slammed the door shut.

***

After trying again to sleep, and pacing for a couple of hours, he came to the conclusion that these guys, this house could only be a distraction. He had to get to the bottom, not by way of a conversation or a phone call, but by sorting it out himself. Time away, he just needed to get away.

He walked around the neighborhood at first, and felt people following him. Could've been sent by anyone—government, Fanya, Roy's network—could have been for various reasons but he was sure people behind him and around corners were keeping a close eye. Could be his death sentence waiting for a certain order of business, or perhaps it was good news! Another party, a surprise party to celebrate the movie deal Roy had in his back pocket since Alex had been pushing that short film years ago.

Or the death sentence.

Could be Roy and Jake were convinced he had done something terrible, because of some kind of set-up Strastikovich designed.

From one minute to the next he was convinced, absolutely convinced of either of these things so he thought his mom might provide a clue about which it was; yet the collect call he made, feigning as if only to inform her of his release, meant she sounded concerned all over again: "Alex, it's five in the morning."

But no time, no time to console her; he had to figure these things out.

The party would be a treasure. Friends from everywhere, long lost favorites of friends all gathered to help him celebrate in the manner of the Kremlin's 48 hours all over again—he would sit like a celebrity being roasted, listening to loving pokes at his eccentric character followed always by an acknowledgement of his creative achievements.

After basking in this scenario, Alex would flip back to his death sentence, and find himself coming to terms to where he wished it would finally happen, just to get on with it—watching from inside the glass of his own lethal injection, while Jake shook his head in sorrow and disappointment, and Roy held Fanya close to comfort her.

He landed at an empty middle-eastern restaurant; turned out Ranalia worked there and brought his wine. She flirted with him and whispered that the wine was on her—more distraction! He had to get out and come to terms.

He found a mid-range priced hotel and checked in. The little Russian man who took his credit card seemed also to be in on the plan with whomever it was keeping tabs on Alex, but he couldn't keep bouncing around anymore; his room would have to offer the solitude he needed.

He called Fanya's number, no answer. He turned the TV on and caught the end of a Russian news story where Roy was signing books and shaking hands with some Russian media personalities; but there was no sign of Jake in the background.

He tried to nap but tossed around while his two possible futures played out for hours, literally hours without a wink of sleep or a step outside.

Late that night he found his way to the hot tub, only an hour before it closed, yet the pool area was occupied by some interesting people, including two American families. There was a grandfather from Texas with maybe half a dozen grandkids splashing around with float-bands and such in the pool. One of the little boys took a dip in the hot tub and so Alex felt he should introduce himself to the grandfather, who was relaxing on a beach chair, and friendly enough to keep Alex feeling easy about staying through to closing.

Soon a couple came in from smoking outside. They were obviously getting smashed; it seemed out of place. The lady was slightly heavy, ass hanging out of her loose boxer style bathing suit bottom, Jamaican accent, loud as hell, passing a paper bag back and forth with her very short, seemingly white-trash boyfriend.

Then Jason, a black athletic dude in his twenties, hopped into the tub following a swim with his white kid brother-in-law, Stephan. They introduced themselves comfortably, and made conversation about their travels. They were there because Jason's wife, a Russian woman, was visiting her family and a great big celebration of some kind was going to take place. Jason wasn't looking forward to it.

The drunk couple left, after a little scene. Alex's shirt was a print of the original poster from *A Clockwork Orange,* and the guy picked it up and blurted something unintelligible about it.

"Put it down!" the Jamaican lady yelled. "It's not your shirt, mon!"

Once they left Jason was none too subtle about his feelings on their departure: "Thank *God*!"

"Kind of a strange couple to find here, right?"
Alex said.

Jason eventually asked Alex what brought him
to Russia, and Alex said he had gone on a
whim, but started dating a woman or he
probably would have been back in the States by
then.

"Ah yeah?" His urban dialect was a breath of
fresh air somehow, very familiar from various
times in Alex's working past. Jason asked, "You
hook up with her here, or from a website?"

"Here."

"Cool, cool. So you can get to know the family
right away. Only thing you gotta think about is
the family. They'll pull you into their shit right
away, believe that."

Stephan sort of chuckled.

Alex turned to the younger brother: "So
Stephan—are you Russian?"

"Nah," Jason offered. "He was born in the
States. He knows what I'm talking about,
though."

Alex was genuinely relieved to be talking to
these people, but he still had an idea that this
was all part of some design. Jason, for example,
could have been a great fit for one of the
characters in the movie from the short he

produced. Alex noticed a video camera above them just over the pool.

When Alex needed a refill he left his room key and said he'd be right back, but he had to come all the way back down and leave again, once he realized he had forgotten it.

He was so enjoying the casual company he hoped dearly they wouldn't leave but maintained a good social front about it: "You all gonna be around a while?"

"Oh yeah. We will close this place down, right Stephan?" and Stephan smiled again.

Upon returning once more, he thanked them for watching his stuff. "Yeah," Jason said casually, "we noticed you left that key; we kept an eye out. Like if that crazy Jamaican bitch came around again or whatever, but we've got your back. I didn't know," he said playfully, "I would've said something but I thought, 'Maybe he's got someone in the room.'"

"No no, I just came for a little time to myself."

"Cool. Kicking back, catching a little you-time. Soaking…"

Stephan then whispered something of concern, but Jason felt no need to hide the conversation. He spoke to Stephan, while pantomiming someone sinking into the tub from a sitting position, "He'd have to be pretty tired to just sink right into the tub," and he pantomimed it again, comfortably, good humouredly.

Why would these guys be looking out for Alex to be drowning in the tub? He felt an easy buzz, but nothing as to cause a watery hot-tub death.

Next there were headlights outside and Jason jumped up. "Oh—that's that thing, I'll be right back," he told Stephan.

Feeling awkward for conversation without Stephan's older brother-in-law there for several minutes, Alex asked about how he and Jason came to be so close.

"It was a video game. At first when he moved in with us, I didn't really know what to think of him, but we started playing 'Crash Bandicoot,' and that's when we started getting along really good."

Jason got back and Alex didn't feel inclined to ask what the car was all about, even though he was curious, suspicious even that it related to him somehow. Alex also confessed in the course of their on and off chatting that he wasn't entirely sure he had kept any geographical track of his location compared to where he was living. Jason immediately got his smart phone out and punched in the cross-streets of the squat-pad, offering an explanation of how to get back Alex was sure he could hang on to until morning.

"Well," Alex said, "I'm gonna turn into a pumpkin." This was a joke that came from Roy, back when Roy, Jake and Tatiana were all crashing together, and Roy was just getting his start. Referring to oneself in the context of a Cinderella story was just the kind of emasculating self-denigration Roy's circle indulged in, and didn't seem like something a stranger should be able to pick up on right away, yet Jason nodded and smiled too quickly, so that it almost seemed he had heard that joke before.

"Enjoy your vodka," Jason said with the same smile.

Alex mused back, "So you're onto me."

"Oh yeah."

"Well I hope nobody else is," Alex said, with an ironic look around the facility.

"We do too."

25.

Days later, Alex had given up on any more conversations about those nights he supposedly spent at the Kremlin. His roommates were both experts in elusive conversational tactics, and so questions never led anywhere, and Alex finally resolved that the Glaring Inconsistencies were going to have to be put aside until next he spoke with Jake somehow. It was time to face more relevant issues moving forward with his life in Moscow.

While Alex was ill-equipped to let go of details like these as a habit, one household item took over as a daily nuisance Alex could no longer ignore—Nicolai. The latest problem revolved around music in the house, and had Alex wondering if he was giving the man more or less credit than he deserved. For example, Alex could name several bands he liked quite a bit, whose hits were not only lower on his list of favorite songs, but on a short list of songs by the same bands Alex didn't care for at all.

Bob Marley's, "Three Little Birds," was one such recording Alex preferred to never hear.

Within moments of admitting to Nicolai and YJ that he didn't care for "Three Little Birds" in the least, Nicolai had it on to repeat, for what seemed to Alex to be an unreasonable amount of time for a joke. Nicolai was singing and dancing about on tables and chairs, seemingly as if in hopes that he might get his two roommates to sing along.

The next morning, as Alex was giving up arguing with his bladder, so badly did he long to stay in bed and urinate simultaneously, Nicolai was blasting "Three Little Birds" again by the time Alex got done in the bathroom and flushed, at which point he stormed into the living area, prepared for confrontation, saying, "Off! Turn that fucking song off! I understand the joke, it was funny once, but *enough!*"

Nicolai seemed genuinely confused: "Easy Alex—did you say you don't like 'Three Little Birds?' I don't remember that, but never mind, relax, I'll only play it while you're at work."

Alex could not determine for himself whether Nicolai was playing an ongoing game or just too drunk or stupid to remember such things, even though it most certainly then became an ongoing theme of an entire obnoxious week leading up to Alex finally moving out. It was then Nicolai presented Alex with a mixed CD including every single song Alex said he hated in those conversations: David Bowie's "A Space Oddity;" Soundgarden's "Black Hole Sun" and "Spoonman" back-to- back; Pink Floyd's "Another Brick in the Wall Part II," right into "Stairway to Heaven" and on it went. When Alex laughed, looking over the songs Nicolai listed meticulously, Nicolai seemed again genuinely surprised: "No, it's not a joke Alex. I just thought it might be something to remember your days here with us."

If it was a joke even YJ was speaking up for it now, saying, "It's true. Squatting has a way of bringing to life that most primal center of the human spirit. It is the ultimate declaration of insisting on survival that urban humans can experience, and even though Nicolai is an idiot, a numbskull, and even though it's possible he may have put this collection together to reveal his dingle-berry infested little ass to you, it stands to reason that at some point you will be glad to hear this CD—maybe next year, maybe next week..."

But Alex wasn't buying any of it: "Gentlemen," pretending to get choked up, "I don't know what to say. Hold me, Nicolai, just put the damn CD in, hold me, and tell me everything is going... to be okay."

Walking out though, he did feel that slightly bittersweet emotion he felt most times when moving. He was an expert at keeping few enough belongings to move easily, and back in the States he would almost always feel the same pangs. It was like he had to give up on a certain dream, a particular idea of what he might have either considered ideal, or maybe just livable, but either way he was giving something up whenever he left a place.

He would especially miss the frequent chats with old man Yellow Jacket.

Placing his third and last box of things into Ranalia's car, he even thought fondly on the evening that bought him his ticket out of the squat house:

YJ was screaming to overpower Nicolai's voice: "What is one house from another? What is one government from another? You give up your shoes willingly, or they take them from you on the street, or in your own home, what difference does it make? You eat your shoes, they will make you regret that too!"

Alex was trying to keep the rhythm of the conversation going, having lost track of the analogy and caught sight of Fanya approaching from a cab outside the window: "Well, so the key is eating someone else's shoes, and having no conscience about it whatsoever perhaps?"

"Yes," YJ was suddenly calm, looking back and forth between Alex right there in the house, and Fanya, now almost to the front door. Before Alex got home from a job, YJ, Nicolai and the other guy he didn't catch the name of had obviously taken some stimulants, or maybe even hallucinogenics, and soon beside Alex were two, then three grown men with bulging eyes contributing to a very uncomfortable welcome to Fanya's approach. They kept staring out the window as Alex got to the door.

He stepped outside, and she greeted him formally, as she was actually on the job and wanted to see him for just a minute. The light kiss was simply to protect her lipstick, though for Alex this was a hard idea to accept considering how intimate they were when she wasn't working. She did say she was there for some kind of reassurance, he couldn't quite understand, before YJ pushed the front door open again, bellowing something in the middle of a spiel about English vs. Scottish pubs.

Nicolai and the guest came out. YJ disappeared then came storming back again having removed one of his shoes so he could wave it furiously at alternating members of the party, to better illustrate his political point, "Eat my fucking shoe you assholes!"

While the old man was at a harmless distance from everyone, the guest decided to join in and got too close to Fanya for Alex's comfort, so Alex raised his own hands in front of Fanya for protection, and Nicolai threw his shoe at the guest while the guest was determining whether or not to take Alex's gesture of defense to the next level; and on being hit in the face by Nicolai's, turned and redirected his aggression, tackling Nicolai while YJ went back to the porch, shaking his head casually, though just as wild-eyed as before.

Alex was embarrassed as Fanya pulled him by his shirt around the corner where her cab still waited. "You live with fucking maniacs. It's time you stayed with me. Let's go now. I can have time with you now, let's go to my flat."

As they got into the cab, he found himself putting together a little poem: "Out of the lunatic pen, and into the Lioness's den."

"I'm a lioness? So why did you come with me?"

"Because you are... beautiful, and you have yet to test your claws on me."

She laughed, sitting on the opposite side of the back seat from him: "So?"

He looked at her without much expression. He was conscious of the physical distance between them and still not secure enough in their relationship to know she wouldn't just put a permanent wall up against him at any time.

She slid about a foot closer to him and said, "So you think I'm beautiful. So what? What are you going to do about it?"

"Same thing I always have."

"What's that?"

"Take it in. Take in every detail I can, while I can."

She smiled, slid right up onto his lap, "And which details are you appreciating now?"

"The curves. Not just on your body, but right here, for example," and he touched her face,

"from your jaw to your neck—then from your collarbone all the way around to your bicep. All of these curves," and he touched her thighs and ass as she straddled him vigorously, "there's a poetry to it that matches your personality—and my desires—past, present, and future...desires."

She liked that very much and kissed him and put a finger over his pant zipper. The cab's video camera rotated audibly in their direction. First Alex looked at it, and when Fanya turned and saw what was distracting him, she said, "You can show these fucking cameras your finger, we are doing nothing wrong. These, these are just for lawsuits, go ahead, show your finger for the camera," and he did, and she rewarded his crotch with what was meant to be just a sensual, tactile sample of what awaited him at his new home, but they both got caught up in their passion and she finished him without even reaching into his pants. She tried not to let on but she knew she had, and smiled out the window behind him as if she had just been caught sneaking an extra helping of dessert.

26.

The first two weeks staying at Fanya's he didn't see that much of her, though they kept up with their sex habit most nights, when one was waking up and the other going to bed. His work schedule had him getting into bed a few hours before her. One night he thought he had a full poem written in his head during his cab home from work, but drunk as he was back at the flat, only got as far as to scribble a few lines: "Flailing hands made only to rip at the intangibles; to dig into the unimaginable."

Fanya was reading these lines with a raised eyebrow when Alex awoke, and she put the piece of paper down on the bed stand, then took him for a quick morning tumble.

What many men would consider a desirable liberty—a devilish sexual visitor offset by schedule to allow for very little else other than sex—Alex found himself begrudging as his feelings for her grew expansively. He was therefore very happy to finally get some days off, resulting in waking time with her. They were already comfortable enough as a couple to laugh behind her clients' backs after sessions, and so she began sometimes calling him from their phones. It was around this time when Alex started listening to the CD Nicolai made. Though suspicious it was intended to disrupt his mental well-being, he sometimes got to feeling morbid enough about his situation—

waiting for a woman he had profound feelings
for, to come back from the beds of others—to
use the CD as an ironic point of reference
regarding his sanity.

One day he was on the phone with Fanya when
he discovered the last song on the CD had
nothing to do with the theme— songs Alex
admitted disliking by artists he liked. She was
whispering to him that the silly old Russian
man had been so easy to please that she had
much more left for Alex than she thought he
could handle. The song came on while she kept
whispering—it was a gut wrenching non-
sequitur he heard through Fanya's expensive
speakers; a choral version of Leonard Cohen's
"Halleluiah," with what he thought was either a
young girl, or a falsetto boy singing the last
verse, about walking floors and all manner of
things children oughtn't know or sing about at
all; and Fanya was insisting that she existed all
the while in Alex's other ear, "I will tease you
for such a long time—you won't know whether
to come or die." And Alex felt such a distinct
sense of elevation, as if he were floating not out
of his body, but in it above the earth, while
hearing her and the choral recording as an
ensemble. This lasted the conversation and
then another ten minutes or so and afterward
he tried to get the experience back by replaying
the song and thinking back on the
conversation, but only got a lightheaded
residue of disorientation, not so much off the
ground, but hovering along from room to room
as he tried to keep that fine line in his drinking

between fending off nervousness and getting too drunk to handle his side of Fanya's plans for him. When she arrived he was nervous, but then ravenous as her teasing was a specialty, and one she claimed to reserve for whomever she was keeping tied up in her bedroom.

And she used an orange and white silk scarf to tie his hands to the bedboard, a black scarf to cover his eyes; then used her tongue and fingers to keep him guessing about what was going to happen next. Once finally inside her he felt those orgasmic pulsations in her, unmistakably, and soon again she came with him mildly after he finished.

"Do you like to eat your women, to eat them out?"

"Sure," he said, head spinning.

"I liked the way you did me; I liked it before, when we were with the other woman. Ana was it? We'll try that in a while, yes?"

"Sure, anything you want," he said, and she laughed coarsely.

27.

For another period of time when they weren't seeing each other or going out, Alex actually gave up drinking, making up for the endorphins with fly-by-morning sex, and even a bit of running and walking in the early evening, before he went to one of Anton's clubs to mix sound.

But when the two of them started going out together regularly as an after party to her work nights, he felt very much inclined to resume drinking. These parties were at places her clients would never be—back room lounges to pricey restaurants specifically designed, it seemed, for Fanya and her girlfriends to drink in the very late evening to early morning after work. The sound of Fanya's voice telling stories in Russian, and cackling wickedly at God knows whose expense was fairly lyrical to Alex's ear, and everyone seemed to treat him well when they knew he was her boyfriend.

One night he felt slight of appetite and ordered a salad. Fanya was in the restroom and the waiter put Fanya's salad down on her side of the table, but then placed an entire duck platter down in front of Alex.

A friend of Fanya's in the corner, named Nika, came and introduced herself, as the platter was meant for her and some friends on the way. Without prompting, Nika very sincerely said,

"I've heard about you. I'm very happy for Fanya—she has been needing something like this. For a long time she has needed you. You came just in time for her."

When Fanya got back she waved Nika away jeeringly, "Don't listen to her. Her kind should not to be trusted. Not just that she's a wanton whore—with her there's no code—no code among the whores with her."

But Alex started to realize he was leaning rather recklessly back on his drinks whenever he started to feel disenfranchised by this sometimes enjoyable environment, and he liked the excuse; he very much liked having a really solid excuse to drink, like when she left him inside one of these very remote restaurants for quite a long time so she could take her call from Anton away from Alex's ear. Later that same evening he was so loose he jumped on stage during some Japanese couple's karaoke rendition of David Bowie's "Ashes to Ashes," when it got to his favorite part of the song. He put an arm around each one of the surprised looking couple, kissed the old Japanese lady and belted without reserve.

Then Fanya even handled him under the table to demonstrate her approval of his enthusiastic spontaneity. After all that, he still felt the sting, from her earlier conversation with the boss that couldn't have him in earshot for some reason. And he went with a room key to get a bottle of wine from an upstairs room, as the bartender

was so impressed by his short outburst of a
performance, they got to talking and he said
Alex must taste this wine, he would love it. So
Alex marveled at the ritzy Russian interior
along the way, even especially in the elevator
itself, then found the bottle in the bartender's
room with some difficulty. He got turned
around just outside of the room, found his way
to another elevator, but it went up to the floor
above him first, and in walked Nika who
wouldn't look up as they were both coming
back down, probably because it appeared she
had been crying for some reason.

And as the sting of having felt left out by
Fanya's phone call to her pimp continued to
linger in a vague way, so had something gotten
to Nika that evening, something probably out of
Alex's scope of understanding, maybe to do
with *her* boss, and Alex found he was asking
her if she was okay, not once but three times,
and "Are you sure?" as he leaned toward her a
little, and she took a friendly step back,
nodding her head that she was sure.

To Alex, drinking was the ultimate act of his
own nihilistic vanity, and he was now keenly
aware of this having been sober in the States,
and relapsed just before moving to Russia. In
his act of drinking, he felt an infinite
expression of disdain for life and self-
indulgence in alienation from it, yet Fanya, God
bless her, Fanya saw through this instantly, and
validated the man that lived behind it all as
well. It sickened him to think that after years of

not searching, but waiting for a woman who might see past his arrogance, Fanya seemed to understand him; and then just recently, having found her, he felt liable to betrayal by essentially making a pass at a good friend of hers in an elevator just because he felt left out of a conversation he probably wouldn't have wanted to hear if he could have. He laughed, leaving the elevator with Nika in front of him; he laughed so lost in these thoughts that Nika joined him, quite puzzled by his behavior.

Then with a glance at Fanya, who was smoking and crinkling her eyebrows regarding why Nika and Alex were returning at once, the short walk back to the table put Alex's stomach in a knot again. To Nika, the virtual pass was presumably a non-issue—but then such a non-issue that she might mention it, at which point Alex might try too hard to brush it aside, casting a darker light on him than Fanya would ever bother to consider.

Soon enough they were finishing the bottle Alex brought down with him, and finally Nika looked at Alex and smiled across the table in such a way as to show that she appreciated his earlier concern, and if things were different, then he might have been able to help; or that's what he thought he saw in her quick smile.

Slowly, sinkingly, Alex began to think that this encounter in the elevator with Nika was a sign that his own, very skewed sense of balance had finally been badly disrupted. He found himself trying to find comfort by thinking back on one of YJ's rants; but it was just a night or two ago, when Nicolai told Alex over the phone that old man Yellow Jacket completely disappeared from the squat pad, and neither could he be found by calling any of the previous numbers where YJ was staying, before the three of them lived together in the house.

28.

"You know it will get cold here, right?"

"I've been dreading that very thing."

"In here," pointing at the entrance to a sports clothes shop. Walking in behind him she added, "Since you are such a... what's the word I'm looking for, when you are not so masculine about something?"

"A wimp? Yes it's true," he offered. "I'm a wimp about cold."

"No, I was thinking of another word. <u>Pussy</u>? Yes, you are a <u>pussy</u> about the cold," and she grinned maliciously while fingering through a rack of impressive jackets with liners, and clips at the sleeves for gloves.

Such cheap shots at his manhood did cut deeper than with any other woman he could think of, who had enjoyed teasing him. It occurred to him that Ana was never one to insult his masculinity verbally; instead she flattered him with words, such as, "You have such a way with women," and then left him doubting her sincerity by choosing the other man.

Such teasing by Fanya hurt, strangely, but it was even more easily repaired by her uttering base compliments and then kissing him: "That one, the thermal shirt you had on earlier. That one is cute. Brings to mind the idea of ripping it off. Put that one in the cart. Yes you are sexy. Let's go pay for your clothes and get home, before I fuck you here in the display window."

Over time, Alex decided that walking and biking through Moscow suited him like no other job he ever had. Fanya wrapped him up with insulation he never knew possible, and stylish outfits at that.

Most places he arrived, he was offered drinks. He didn't know what it was, the drug he delivered, always to the dealers, never to the clients (this was the stipulation Fanya argued for, and adamantly, on Alex's behalf), but he enjoyed presenting a joke to each new dealer that offered him a drink. While toasting he would always say, "This is the part of my job I am *over*qualified for. How do you say that in Russian, 'Overqualified'?"

One morning he woke up and Fanya wasn't letting him touch her. He asked what was wrong and she said, "If you don't remember I can't talk to you right now," and left.

He continued to learn about Russian firearms by going to the shooting range with Nicolai and sometimes a couple of Nicolai's friends. Soon Alex was doing more work running sound at Anton's clubs than he was muling. He got slightly closer to Anton, and one night Anton opened up to Alex surprisingly. He was drunk, but appeared more open than Alex was used to seeing him. His guard was down; he almost seemed vulnerable: "I have lost her."

"What?"

"You know, she's yours. I loved her at one time."

"You? You're the... the Tzar around here, you can't be serious."

"No," he took a smoke, "I loved her, in a way that I can't and do business, and I saw when you came that I had to choose between love and business."

"I'm...well thanks for telling me, I guess."

Anton took a drink of beer, wiped his long gray moustache and his beard, "I have thought about it, I have been watching you two, more than you realize," and the smile was as insidious as the implication, "and I decide she will stay."

"Stay?"

"In Russia—I will not sell her to Thailand, or to Amsterdam. To watch you two makes me sad, but it is better, it's better to keep this feeling close. It makes me remember what is important—*zhertva. Da.* Sacrifice."

She got back and he was drunker than the night before, but broken up by her statement. He tried so hard to remember while she was gone the entire night. He took no jobs at all, just sat there trying to think to himself what happened, and what he would have to do to win her trust again. He shuddered many times over the prospect of having hit her. He couldn't believe he had it in him. Though he did remember arguing.

"So Anton, you were saying that, I mean do you often take those kinds of deals from the south, for girls I mean?"

"Yes. I might still, with Fanya. We'll just see how you work out. You keep remembering, you may have won the girl, but I'm still the boss. I can always make a deal for her, so you should always be looking to get the best deal for me."

"Fanya, don't tell me that you're tired. I'm a wreck, there's no way I'm going to sleep unless you tell me what happened."

"Nothing. Nothing happened. We argued, men and women do that, since the day one we have and will always fight, forget it!"

Alex broke to tears, "I can't. I can't forget; you have to tell me."

Her grammar was broken, as was common when she was distraught: "Fine. We fight. I want you to take me to United States, you don't want to go. I tell you something, something mean, something to reject you, but never mind, I tell you and I turn around and you are this close to hitting me," and she showed him the space between her pointer finger and her thumb, "This close. But me, I count myself lucky woman, I count myself this lucky," and she showed him how lucky she was with those same fingers, very close to his face, then retreated for a cigarette.

After a while he broke the silence, "So, why did I tell you I didn't want to go?"

"It doesn't matter. I know you. I know you well enough. You don't want to go. I believed you when you almost hit me, you don't want to go back."

"But most of all," Anton said, then sucked his own pointer finger grotesquely, "Most of all, *zaromni*—I can still get a taste of her. *Boodoo kapshatz,* I will be tasting of her."

Fanya walked in as Anton was leaving the table. Anton gave her an exaggerated kiss "*Privyet*" to underline his cold point to Alex. Fanya was back from a funeral—that of her *Babushka*. Held north of them, she had no interest in seeing her family, but did love her Babushka and also was uncertain as to how the house would be split up between her and her brothers. A good deal of money went to the brothers, but she inherited the cabin, and a car.

Alex was broken up over what Anton said and couldn't hide it from her. Fanya's recent run-in with Alex's clay feet in a drunken rage of an argument was not sitting well with her, and so with her *Babushka* dead, she had little to give to Alex in the way of reassurance. "Yes," she said. "It is what the pimps do. They sell us."

They were up on the second floor sitting at a table near the soundboard. On the stage below them across the large room, there was an accordion and violin duet engaged in a sound check, though Alex's work for them was essentially done. There were no other people in the club, yet Alex began to feel a strange momentum, as if the show had already started and he and Fanya would get up to dance, though Alex was aware that he himself had no dancing skills. The violinist began playing a painfully romantic solo, lending an excruciating irony to the listlessness of his love's posture and tone. It was so tense between them that Alex found himself looking around for something to focus his frustration on, afraid of the consequences should he pursue anything further with Fanya. He spotted Anton's scarf left behind, on the chair across from him, but that was too close to the topic so next he noticed that right in front of him, on the table where they were sitting was an antique skillet. It seemed out of place so he said, "What the fuck is this?"

She didn't even look back in his direction, said, "What the fuck is what?"

He tapped impatiently, "This, right here, why is this here?"

"It's an… old skillet, who cares, why are you so upset?"

"It's just odd, out of place."

"Well throw it away," she said pointedly, referring back to an argument about a letter Alex received from Ana. "No one will notice, just throw it away."

"What I want to do is crack Anton across his miserable skull with it."

"Well," she said casually, "I did just get this car. It's not even in my name yet."

Before the solo ended Alex heard footsteps coming up the stairs and had the skillet clutched in his hand. Fanya laughed at first, but then Anton turned their corner and was unconscious after the second hit, but by no means was Alex finished once Anton was asleep. The blood only got on Fanya's leather purse; she did away with that using a napkin and then took Anton's scarf and started working on cleaning Alex up. She was calm and clear: "What have you done? We must walk out of here. I was joking, love. It's okay, we will leave and you must be cool. Cooler than I have ever seen you," and she presented a strange smile with that. "You must be very, very fucking cool." Then she broke her own cool, and looked at him closely, touched his face: "*Shto vui stalali*, Alex? What have you done?" and she held him tight and kissed him hard, then touched him softly on the face again as if he were a child.

Before that fight there was the matter of a letter from Ana. Fanya kept asking him if he wanted her to open it until Alex got irritated and Fanya defensive. He was also uncomfortable about it because he never mentioned to Fanya the time he bumped into Ana and had a few conversations with her at the Kremlin, and he was afraid there might be some mention of that. He said, "I don't trust her, I'm sorry. Please—let's just keep what we've got between us. I can deal with your work, but we're at home now. Just you and me, Fanya, please."

"And why should I not think you want to open it when I'm not around?"

"Throw it away."

"It's not my mail to throw away. And I don't want you to throw it away, I just want to open it."

"No."

"Fine. I'm going."

"It's what you do. I'll see you for dinner."

29.

Alex woke up in the car having lost touch
emotionally with the reason they were running.
He knew the extent of it, but with a nap
managed to somehow put the situation aside
and take interest in conversation between the
two of them.

"Fanya—how much time did you spend with
your *Babushka*, when you were younger?"

"Oh, normal, you know, visits. But for a while I
saw her more, we were living closer. The cabin.
The cabin we had when I was little girl, so there
are lots of memories."

She told her brothers she was renting the cabin
out, and changed the land-line number so she
and Alex wouldn't be bothered with their
coming by and asking them for money, once
the brothers' part of the inheritance ran out.
Alex enjoyed bringing wood in, and there was
much already cut but he even started chopping
up logs from some of the cruder piles at the
back of the land. Anywhere near the
surrounding fence, if he dug he'd find plastic,
and wrapped in that plastic was wood needing
to be cut. He would cut wood picturing her
face, and sorting through plans he couldn't see
happening, like their moving together to some
small town elsewhere in Europe or even Asia,
and starting fresh and becoming as married,
even if just for a time, what did he care? He

loved her, he'd already written everything else off, and as Yellow Jacket once said, that was that. He would give what he had, same as with any love; why think of this differently? But it was only unrealistic for one reason—the main earner of the household wasn't working any more than he was.

Even when it was snowing outside, time would fly by while he was outside chopping wood. The snow in his face and the sweat inside those many layers of clothes marked Alex's contribution and entitlement to a hot drink with Fanya at the end of the day.

Throughout their cohabitation in the cabin, Alex was generally flipping back and forth between two assumptions: the first being that she utterly resented him for having taken her away from her life in Moscow, as lowly a life as that may have seemed to him; the second that she was grateful that Alex had gotten her out of the business, but suffered from restlessness where they were. While he realized that their isolation, combined with moodiness they both were prone to had more to do with Alex's interpretation of the situation than whatever was going on in her head, he felt it would be foolish to dig for an answer about how she felt, no matter what time of the day or how they were getting along. *Babushka*'s cabinets were full of food and liquor, and the nearest store, further north, seemed to be run by people completely unaware of city-life. When Alex went into town he would make sure to hide his features in the very believable guise of clothing protecting him from the elements.

They kept the gun Fanya stole from Anton on their way out of the club in a drawer by the front door, and Alex was quick to produce it when he heard cars, or even animals moving about, which made Fanya sometimes tense, and sometimes more at ease. She told him he was too easily startled, but also quietly appreciated the fact that he was on the look out whenever he was awake. One day at sunset he went out after a sound and it was a pack of wolves, having stolen a beaver carcass, or something about that size. Alex had a moment with the last, beautiful gray wolf to leave Fanya's property. He stood quietly staring directly into its eyes. The animal's heckles were up slightly, but it seemed caught there. When it finally left, after maybe thirty or forty seconds, Alex recalled the wolf that Nicolai killed right before Alex started dating Fanya.

When Alex returned, he didn't even mention the wolves. The fire was truly blazing, Fanya was in a certain mood, it seemed Alex might be allowed to enjoy the sort of time he remembered with her those weeks before they fought about Ana's letter. Fanya's tender eyes watched as he intently shook and removed his boots, hung his jacket, made his way finally back inside the living room and put the gun away. Next they were intertwined as in young love and Alex was staring at the fire. His head cocked at another sound, and Fanya put her hands over his ears. He heard his voice enclosed in his head while he asked her, "What are you doing that for?"

"I want you to hear no evil."

"Where is the evil coming from?"

"I don't know. It could turn up anytime."

He turned around and kissed her and she leaned back and took him in her arms and whispered, "Remember the old man that used to talk to us at your house with that other guy, the bonehead?"

"Yeah. Yellow Jacket, we called him. I miss him."

"I do too. That was fun."

"Well it was a strange place to live."

She turned her head to the side, coughed, glanced at the fire, then looked right back at him, "But it had its place, at the beginning for us. That house served its purpose when we were just starting to get to know each other. I used to get a thrill on my way over there to see you. Did I ever tell you that?"

"Yeah. But on my end, I kept thinking it would be the last time you'd come and visit—each time I pretty much took it for granted, that it was the last time I would see you."

She was impish in bed afterward. She wouldn't give him a second to relax, immediately she'd be wrestling with him or jabbing at him before she just started pouring out information he would have had to spend a fortune on booze to get out of her otherwise.

He just kept going back outside to cut wood. Cabin fever has Fanya a little wound up? Head out to cut wood. Alex feeling a little insecure after a less vocal orgasm from Fanya despite his greatest efforts in cunnilingus? He would go cut wood. Running out of wood to cut? He found a saw and fell or severed small and fallen trees to a manageable size—to create more wood to chop. Only by working all day in the dreaded snow did he find he could predictably clear his mind of everything but the look on her face when the carpet was laid out and she was actually glad to be stranded out in the woods with him.

One afternoon she brought home some high-end champagne a customer had forgotten all about. While they were frolicking and drinking, she kept making as if to say something, then pulling back. Finally she broke down and started touching his hair and looking right at him: "When you were in the hostel. You remember?"

"About a day ago?"

"Shut up—you remember, okay, so when you used to tell stories, had everyone laughing about

how you left the States and this kind of thing, remember?"

"Vaguely. Yeah. I didn't really..."

"Shut up! I'm talking." They laughed, she continued. "Do you remember seeing people on the outskirts, looked probably overdressed?"

"Yeah. I figured they were Anton's guys, right?"

"Yes, yes they were Anton's guys. How many did you see?"

"Oh, one or two. I don't know."

"Yes they were Anton's guys, but Anton did not send them."

"Oh?"

"No. I sent them." She covered her mouth. "I sent people to spy on you. That's how curious I was. I wanted to know things, but I didn't want you to know I was interested, and so I paid them some money. I am the one who was trying to get you closer to Anton. Anton may have been jealous, but that didn't mean he was interested in you. It was me." She giggled and said a rhyme in Russian that started with her fingers as two horns moving in circles, and ended with those horns in his belly. They rolled around on the bed, then the floor, and kept playing like that until Alex had to go to the bathroom.

248

*"I punch you so hard you almost pissed pants!
Pussy!" she yelled at him from the bedroom to
the bathroom.*

*Later they were mellow, drinking the last of the
champagne, when Fanya brought it up again:
"But I wouldn't have had the nerve to…
approach you if Ana hadn't paid. There's no
way I would have ever gotten you to date me if
Ana hadn't been so bold as to set us up."*

"Well, for that alone, I thank her."

"That alone?"

"Yes."

*They locked hands where they laid, looked into
each other's eyes, and Alex could swear that was
more intimacy than Alex had experienced in his
lifetime.*

30.

Alex came in after about an hour of work. He was tired of it. They had enough wood and it was obvious—it was positively stacked up against the cabin and along the fences beyond the realm of imaginary need given any length of winter. The food was taken care of by Fanya. He had no idea what the money situation was and that was fine with him. It was the same way in the city—she took care of money, he took care of her; or at least they both pretended he was taking care of her.

She had a spark in her eye that frightened him at first. He recalled the blackout, having almost hit her back in Moscow, and knew he couldn't go out very far away from the cabin if he felt on the edge of losing it. If she was in a mood, in some kind of haughty mood ready to bring a storm of arguments in, he just didn't trust himself that day, it all felt too precarious.

Instead of poking at him subtly, about the snow he tracked in, or the fact that they didn't need any wood and he was as useless to her there as he had been in the city, or how could he possibly have made such a decision as to sever her from her occupation?—or countless other possible triggers to threaten his last reasons for being her boyfriend, or being anyone at all, she said, "We have been in too long. It's time we went out!"

Alex stood looking at her dumbly for several seconds and she savored every moment, then interrupted her own enjoyment as if in self-sacrifice: "And you are wondering how? You wonder if your sweetheart has gone completely crazy?"

"No, I just thought we were keeping a low profile."

He hadn't noticed that Fanya's hands were behind her back; she brought them forward with a tall, thin box clenched in both fists, and a proud smile on her face. He stepped forward and caught on to her thinking immediately. The truth was, he had nothing to go on regarding what would be safe for the two of them and what wouldn't, and he didn't care—his cabin fever was at least as severe as hers and she could have shown him a little dolly from her childhood and said it was a good omen and he would have been just as convinced they ought to go out that door in seconds, but what she had was a box of hair dye.

Alex enjoyed the attention it required for Fanya to take him through the process of applying the stuff, and just like that his hair was black. That was their entire disguise from the law, and the organized crime syndicate alike—both had reasons to take them out, and Alex's black hair was to open the door to a night of frolicking in public as if they never made a wrong turn against either very powerful, and presumably somewhat interrelated entity.

In the car Fanya explained: "There is a bar my brothers used to take me to, when we were staying with *Babushka* here. We only got caught once, and she whipped my brothers, but she didn't whip me!" and she cackled.

"Not by the store. I would have seen it, I've driven all over."

"No, no it's further up. All it says on the sign is *Restoran.* I already called to make sure it still open. It's a little tiny place with a pool table. You have to show me about these 'house rules' you were telling me about."

Right then a flood hit Alex from his past. He hadn't been able to imagine calling Jake. What would he tell him? This was not a call from jail asking for a ride, he was a fugitive, and putting any number that could be traced back to Alex into that cabin phone seemed idiotic. It surprised Alex that Fanya still used the phone at all.

When they walked into the bar, Alex was immediately at ease. Even though the old couple that owned it knew Fanya by sight, they were calling her by another name, he didn't quite catch it, something like Mariana; but he couldn't imagine they were in touch with Moscow society, and anyway, the sight of a bar was like water to a man in the desert at that point. He started with an old favorite: cheap scotch on the rocks, whatever they had in the well.

Fanya caught on to Jake's "house rules," meaning basically no called shots and the harder you hit the better; she caught on very quickly and enthusiastically. Alex actually had to dodge the cue ball, or other random balls flying off of the table as a result of Fanya's enthusiasm now and again.

Then Alex was sent back into the realm of Glaring Inconsistencies, when a couple walked in he thought at first to be wearing some strange undergarments that covered most of their faces. As they drew closer, Fanya was digging her knuckles into Alex's leg, and shaking her head very subtly for reasons that became clear during their second or third game of doubles pool against the couple, once they both happened to need the restrooms at the same time Alex assumed Fanya was trying to make sure he wouldn't stare at the deformity they shared: a more severe case of what the police officer had—the one who finally set Alex free from the Glendale jailhouse what seemed an eternity ago. The man and the woman, a pleasant couple it turned out, were overrun by long, thin facial and neck hair, and once the jackets were off he could see it covered their arms as well. But this wasn't what Fanya was nudging Alex about at all.

Their names were Bonnie and Andrei. Fanya finally whispered, after acting entirely embarrassed on their behalf for a long, uncomfortable stretch: "Bonnie is *not from Russia*," and Alex just couldn't believe this was Fanya's main point about the two of them, though he never brought it up to her that night or thereafter. Alex found he could hardly keep a straight shot, so distracted was he by their appearances, until he and Fanya lost pretty badly, for a couple of games in a row. It was then Alex found a rare run of attention span for the game of pool.

While Alex was on this roll, he did very much enjoy the affection this brought from Fanya, who was behaving more competitively than he had ever seen her. He vaguely recalled a couple of doubles games back in Moscow with her and asked how they did back then.

"We were good," she shrugged. "We were good team. You always played like shit when you were playing against me, and I figured you were throwing those games. Were you?"

"Probably not. I was probably just drunk." And honesty at past ineptitudes he barely recalled bought him the same thing high performance in the current game had—affection. It was a good night for Alex.

He slowed down on the drinks when Fanya started to show signs of sleepiness, thinking he would have to drive and they were at least forty miles from the cabin; but the furry couple left them alone again with the owners, who insisted

they should stay in a little room they kept
available in the basement for just such nice
people as Fanya and Alex.

31.

They started coming to the bar about twice a week. After a while, Fanya was offered a shift on occasion. Alex was helping the owners, Petr and Guana, in small ways around their house. The house was about a half a mile down the mostly barren highway from the bar. There were some technological challenges Alex thought of as fairly remedial, like a new computer that had been sitting around for about a year as best as he could understand. Petr and Guana were actually from Georgia originally, and used some strange expressions he couldn't quite catch on to.

When he got to know Guana fairly well, he even started hinting about the possibility of bringing live music to their bar, and Guana seemed interested but the conversation probably never made it as far as a chat with Petr. Their memories were getting slow, and their ambitions even slower with grandchildren as far away as Tbilisi, and ambiguity regarding the fate of the bar and their house once they passed away.

After the computer was up and running, there was always something new they wanted to try and do with it, such as watch a DVD of their grandchildren playing around with a camera, or send group emails out, and many things they needed more than one tutorial on and so it seemed that there might always be a drink credit waiting for him at the bar, even if Fanya wasn't the one on shift.

But after a few weeks there was a visit from some of their offspring, and a few of their grandchildren as well, and Fanya said she heard them in the back-room of the bar arguing over Alex's work for them, claiming that they shouldn't be paying anyone that much for what he was doing, and that they could have shown them how to do all of that on a video chat (which of course the old couple never would have been capable of before Alex started working for them). In short, the Georgian family was trying hard to convince their parents that Alex was taking advantage of them.

His next appointment with them was made before the family came to visit, and turned out to be one of very few remaining appointments at all. They would make excuses, and Alex felt entirely incapable of challenging the family's accusations against Alex and the value of his work with them. He felt that after all what they wanted was company, and continued to think so even once they stopped calling on him, and Fanya said that she would look for opportunities to address the subject, but the truth was Alex enjoyed keeping the fire going back at the cabin during Fanya's shift just as much as he liked making a few bucks at Petr and Guana's house. When Fanya's shift was short enough, he could even go with her, drop her off, take a lunch at the ski resort a little way's east of the bar, then come back and sip a cocktail with Fanya after she handed the place over to some very worn looking barmaid Alex never quite learned to call by name.

One day Fanya took a half day ticket to go skiing and didn't even mention it to Alex. He was trying to hide his dejected feelings upon hearing of it after the fact, when she managed to corner him logically, saying, "Would you have wanted to go?"

"No," and he laughed, but he was still crestfallen. "Well, maybe. Is there a spot from inside the lounge where I can see you coming down the hill through a window?"

"No."

"Well, maybe not, maybe not, but ask next time will you?"

"*Da. Sleduyutsi raz,*" she said, and started to whisper "Next time" but was cut off.

"*Spacibo,*" Alex said, without realizing he had thanked her in Russian.

32.

For a while Alex tried sticking to beer, but it was awkward buying that much beer from the little stores they were patronizing. The toll vodka took on him was usually fairly predictable and manageable, but one evening she asked about that letter from Ana again and he completely lost it. He didn't stand up, but he went on sarcastically in his arrogance, "You're jealous? Seriously, you? You're jealous here?" He looked around the cabin mockingly. "What am I going to do, skip away with a beaver?" She laughed at that, but he carried on unnecessarily until it became another real argument.

Periodically Alex found himself wondering if that was why she seemed distant again, until she called from the airport to tell him she was leaving.

"I'm sorry, I have to go. It's Ana. She offered to help me, to put me up in the States, and I know you don't want to go back or even talk about her. She offered so casually—without knowing where that leaves you…"

With those words Alex was reduced to feeling and speaking like a groveling sixteen year old boy: "Wait, hold on, please. I'm sorry I've been acting strange but… we were doing all right. We can work through… whatever it is, Fanya."

"It's more than that. More complicated."

"What? Tell me; you're always holding back the part I need."

"No, you don't need this."

"What, please, you have to tell me. Tell me what went wrong."

"I've been talking to her. She's not just going to help me, we have come to be talking, I'm sorry, when you went to the store, and we love each other, in our own strange way, there's no way you can understand. She doesn't know she's hurting you, not yet but, there was just no way...I could turn her down."

Alex thought back to when he walked in on Ana and Trenton. Thought back to the moment he slammed Trenton into the heater at the alcoholics gathering on Thanksgiving. And then he thought about the man he just murdered. There was a common thread; he couldn't put his finger on it, but something to this puzzle he still didn't understand.

"I have to go. I'm sorry," she said convincingly. She sounded choked up, but not enough so Alex would have anything to be hopeful about if he ever found her again.

Alex took five full minutes to hang up the phone, despite the noises it made when Fanya was long gone. He went straight to the letter he used to argue with Fanya about. Fanya—the

crazy, abused, beautiful woman he just lost;
she used to be on his case, he laughed thinking
to himself, about an as of yet sealed letter from
Ana.

Ana—who somehow managed to take Fanya
away from him without trying, without even
wanting to, more than likely. He opened it, half
hoping to find some hint of this latest magical
act, but all it said was, "Dear Alex—LOVELY
evening, very strange indeed, I'd expect nothing
less. You should really take this train ride down
to Prague sometime. It's beautiful. Thinking of
you, Ana."

Thanks for reading. Please sign up for a newsletter telling of latest releases by *Seven Eleven Stories* and Barnaby Hazen:

www.sevenelevenstories.com

www.ingramcontent.com/pod-product-compliance
Lightning Source LLC
Chambersburg PA
CBHW072349020726
47506CB00004B/1061